Where

THE White Rose

Withers©

HARELL SMILEY

Where

THE White Rose

Withers©

Unapologetically beautiful, Explicit and Wild

Spin-off of the trilogy *Beautiful Wicked*.

Warning: This novel is inspired by real experiences and stories using heavy drug use.

"Ms. Rose. This is serious. Someone was killed amongst other events that happened. What do you know about it?" The investigator asked. Danielle sat in the chair, arms and legs crossed. "His body was found in the river. Given your recent relationship with the victim, it is important for us to discredit any possible suspects. Please." The investigator slides a picture of the corpse in front of her. A tear fell from Danielle's puffy red eyes. "I want my lawyer." She demands.

1.The spark of a flame.

New York was *very* different from Savannah Georgia. The people were different. Snobbier than the people down south, but this is exactly where Danielle fit in. Leaving their home, friends and loved ones in Savannah Georgia behind was hard. This was a new world for the Rose family. There she is, Danielle Rose. At the front desk of The H Hotel. Her finger twirls around her orange hair. The concierge hands her a copy of the golden elevator key to the penthouse. "Send up the bag boy." Danielle orders, walking to the elevator. "Don't you mean the bags, Miss Rose?" The concierge asked. "I know what I said." Danielle smiles and winks as the elevator closes.

She sits at her vanity, admiring the beautiful image that the Rose lineage has passed down. Her smooth, creamy skin. She moves her long, fire orange hair behind her to put on mascara. "Dani, let's go!"

Nate Rose; her twin brother rushes her. They are spending their last free day in Manhattan before they start their first day of junior year. "Okay, I am coming." She replies, now applying her famous matte, rose red lipstick and then dabs a little powdered foundation on her lips.

"Mother, we are leaving." She yells in the apartment. "Okay be safe you two." Their mother; Hazel Rose, says looking over paperwork. "Dani. Play nice." Felton; their father smiled. Nate and Danielle hopped in the black town car and headed for the big city.

"Dani, we have been shopping all summer and we have yet to make any friends. Well you haven't anyways." He says, focused on his phone. "And who the hell would be friends with you?" She laughs, fixing her makeup. "I don't need friends. I have brothers. I am on the football team." Nate gloated "Oh so you're still a jock head, but I am proud of you." Danielle smiled. As twins, they had to do everything together. They shopped together, ate together, and went out together. They even ruled *The Savannah Grove Prep School* together. "So, are you going to change or still try to rule over the school?" Nate asks with a sinister smirk. "I guess we will see. Expect the unexpected." She returns the smile.

They finally arrive in the Upper East Side. Danielle starts in Bloomingdales and works her way to Barneys, Jimmy choo, Louis V, Burberry, Lord and Taylor even had her nails done.

Nattie: *I am done with my shopping. I will be at the Garden on Madison.*

Dani: *Okay I am finishing up now.*

She finishes her shopping at Saks and heads to The Garden to meet her brother. Danielle struts through the doors and sees him staring at a group of girls. "Pay attention." She snaps her fingers. Her perfectly black claws got his attention. "Woah those are a lot of bags." He says, eyes getting wider. "Well I had to make sure I have nice clothes." Danielle smiles. "You have enough nice clothes Dani." He takes a sip of his Corona. "Well I also have makeup and accessories." She argues playfully. "Who are you looking at?" Danielle turns to get a good look at her face. "This girl just rushed out of the bathroom with the barista guy." Nate whispered. "Which one?" Danielle snuck a peak. "The one that doesn't belong in that group." He whispers, talking about the big girl. Hmm, Spanish, short dark hair and bangs. She wore a diamond "C" on her necklace. The other girl was black with long black hair. She wore a beautiful floral blouse that was tucked into a black pencil skirt. The third girl was leaving. She was a cute innocent girl, blonde. Obviously trying to fit in or lead the group. "Don't be an ass. You asked me if I was going to change or try to take over the school…" Danielle saw an opportunity and strutted over to the girls table. Nate sits back and throws his arm over the seat.

"You girls seem like an interesting group. You all go to school around here?" Danielle asks, taking a seat. "Trish does, the girl that just left. But we attend Oberlin Billard." The girl with the C says. "I am Crystal by the way." She introduced herself, pushing up her vintage glasses. She had a tray of apples and grapes and wouldn't stop Snapchatting, that told Danielle everything she needed to know about her. "And I'm Amber." The other one says with a faint smile that showed she wasn't impressed or interested. "Oh awesome. This will be my first year there. I'm Danielle and my brother Nathaniel. Is there anything I should know about the school?" Danielle leans closer to ask, flipping her hair behind her. "Well the school runs off of hierarchy. After Annabella Dayton, there hasn't been anyone that could take her place. The other girls on the council have to approve." Amber answers. "I had dinner with her, before everything happened to them." Danielle bragged. "You had dinner with Annabella?" Amber didn't believe her. "Okay correction. My dad and her dad are best friends growing up, so our families had dinner together." Danielle corrected. "Well you know what they say, if you want power you must take it. I'm a big believer in expecting the unexpected." Danielle smiles.

The girls exchange numbers and the two head back home in the town car. "So, did you get what you want?" Nate asked. "Not just yet, but I will." She smiles, looking out of the window.

They arrive back at The H Hotel penthouse. It's one of the top three nicest stays in the Hamptons. They stayed on the fortieth floor. Two stories, five bedrooms, two and a half baths. The kitchen was huge, and the living room was bigger. "Are you ready for school tomorrow bud?" Felton pats Nate's shoulder, scaring him a bit. "I am. Can't be afraid of going to a new school. I'm seventeen." Nate picks up the remote off of the floor and balances it on his knee. "What did your coach say about your playing?" Felton folds up a newspaper. Felton was actually interested in knowing about Nate's life for once. "Well he says I play really well and that I can be captain very soon if I put in the work, but he hasn't decided yet." Nate couldn't stop the smile from showing on his face. "Hey dad can-" He is interrupted by a sound of something vibrating. Felton held up a finger and answered the phone call. "Hey Al.

What? They are interested in selling? I am not sorry for what I did. It was a necessary evil. Look, I will be right there." Felton jumps in excitement. "I'm sorry. Did you need anything else?" Felton asked, covering the speaker. "No. Go take care of business." Nate gives him a small smirk and walks off. That attention was short lived. Longer than usual, but still short lived. When it comes to business, family is put to the side apparently.

Here it is. The depression kicking in. Nate was missing his old life. The south. His friends, he could do everything they used to do. Hunting, parties, girls, drinking, sports. Now he has no one. Even his sister is planning to take over. Part of him doesn't want to be just another football star. He just wants to live and be happy with his new start while he still can.

Nate walks into the dining room to find Hazel cooking with the chef. "What is going on here? It smells delicious." Nate claps his hands together. "We have steak going, and veggies and mashed potatoes." The chef; Bonnie answered. "I am just helping. And wine of course." Hazel laughs. "Honey, where is your sister?" Hazel asks. "In her room. Rearranging her closet. She has way too many clothes. It's insane. And dad just went to a business meeting." Nate explained before she could ask. "I'm gonna go explore the building. I will be back in time for dinner." Nate starts for the elevator. "Nate. Stay out of trouble." Hazel yells.

The view from the rooftop is absolutely stunning up here. The city and beach lined up nicely. The ocean waves create a pattern towards the shore. The sun disappeared behind the ocean line. The August air was soothing. "*Just right*" He always liked to say. He takes a deep breath and slowly lets it out. "New here?" A girl asks from the edge. "Yeah. Is it that noticeable?" Nate snickers. "Ginger, nice. Don't see too many of you here." She laughs. "Thanks, well I'm Nate. I just moved here from Georgia. Definitely a change." He walks over to the edge. "I'm Erica Worthington. My family moved back here too." Erica says. Erica was definitely the loner type. Short brown hair, short also, but he could tell she had spirit once you really got to know her. "Back here? What happened? And are you going to Oberlin Billard as well?" Nate plops down next to her. "Actually, that school is why we left. My sister was bullied, and it caused us to move. I go to Stanley Prep. It's a pretty nice elite school. Not Oberlin level. But it is nice." She takes a puff of her cigarette. "Well, my dad is actually trying to buy this building. Since the Dayton family is uh, gone." Nate informed. "Oh, that would be awesome. You would be living here for free, you wouldn't have to worry about anything. Hope you guys are better than them." Erica laughs. "I think we are. From the one time I have met them, I didn't see anything wrong with them." Nate explains. With a flick of his lighter, he lights a joint and takes a puff. "Can I?" She asks holding her hand out. "Sure. Don't trip on me though." He lets out a slight laugh. She took a giant puff and handed it back. "That is some really good stuff." Erica coughs out the words. "Well I hope to see more of you. I gotta go." Nate holds the door open. "Well you know where to find me. Nice to meet you Nate the great." She smiled at him. Those eyes. Something about her. "Nice to meet you Erica the meric..a... bye." Nate rushes into the stairway. "Merica? Come on idiot!" He whispers to himself as he hears the giggle from her.

Entering the apartment, dinner was placed on the table and Danielle was clicking her way in her heels to the dinner table. "You smell, shower and eat before mommy sees you." Danielle flips her hair. Nate dashed upstairs and showered. When he made it back down.

Hazel and Felton joined the table. "Nice to have you. And not smelling up the dining room." Hazel says. "How did you smell it?" Nate asks. "Son, marijuana leaves a very strong-smelling trail." His father explained. "You set me up!" Nate whispered, sitting beside his sister. "You wish you were that important to me." She snaps back. The food smells absolutely delicious. And not because he is high. "What did the sellers say, love?" Hazel asks Felton. "They are putting the process on hold, so we will have a meeting soon with the board and myself. I have nothing to worry about. We will own the hotel and make it legendary." He smiles, chewing his food. "When is Donny coming to visit? I miss him." Danielle asks about her older brother who graduated from Yale. He will be a good lawyer. "I don't know honey. I hope soon. Reach out to him sometime." Hazel sips her wine. "I'm going to get ready for bed. See you guys in the morning." Nate gets up from the seat and heads up to the bedroom.

Sitting on his bed, boxes still everywhere. Thinking about why he couldn't get this girl out of his head. He was never into girls like her. She's not someone he would have near him back in Georgia.

First day of school

Danielle tucks her white, off the shoulder shirt into her red skirt. Her black stockings slide into her heeled grey boots. Orange hair curls down her back. Clip on her choker and grabs her bag. She followed the smell of waffles. "That smells delish!" She sits next to her jock head brother in his button up and shorts and... are those boat shoes? She studies him. "I gotta meet the guys. See you at school!" He put a waffle into his mouth and swung the black book bag over his shoulder and headed to the elevator.

"I did what I did because he denied me of my right." Felton says before seeing Nate. Felton hung up quickly. "Wait son." Felton stops him in midair. "I think you two are responsible enough for these." Felton held out keys. Nate got a matte, dark copper G wagon. And for Danielle, the black Mercedes Benz c300. "No way! Thank you!" Nate nearly jumped into his daddy's arms. "Be safe you two." He says hugging them tight. "Thank you, daddy." Danielle smiles. "This means I have to change shoes." Danielle, now running up to her room. Putting on her thigh high black boots.

New Text Message

Crystal: *Meet us in the courtyard by the knight.*

Danielle makes her way to school. Blasting pop music. Singing along. Driving fast. The long curvy road led her to the parking lot of Oberlin. She steps out of the car and observes the students. All kinds of personalities. All kinds of clothes. All like her. Finally, Danielle enters the outside corridors and sees the courtyard. "Hey hey." She greets, walking up to Amber and Crystal. "You look great. I love those shoes." They complimented. "Thank you. I figured why not impress on the first day right? So why meet here?" Danielle flashes a smile. Nate stands about fifty feet away with his teammates. All so juicy. "That seat is reserved for the Queen and her ladies. That seat could be ours." Amber explained. "Not could. It will be." Danielle corrects. She flutters over to the table and takes a seat. All eyes are now on her. "What are you doing?" Amber asks in shock. "We are taking power." Danielle flashes her famous sinister smile. The girls follow her lead.

Students mumble about these invaders. "Who is that?" "Is she the new Queen of Oberlin?" "I didn't hear anything about it on the Dot." Danielle pulls out her phone. "What is the dot?" She asks. "A site where gossip and news flies faster than TMZ." Crystal shows her the page. "This stuff is interesting. Like *Gossip Girl*. But way more intense." Danielle takes a selfie, blowing a beautiful red kiss to everyone and captioned it *New Queen of Oberlin*. She added her twitter handle and Instagram name and sent it. Moments pass and everyone sees it.

Morning Oberlin, I woke up this morning and found a beautiful Rose growing in my garden. Definitely Queen material. We will see if she has what it takes.

Love TheDot.com

Danielle stands on the table and looks over everyone. "Hello everyone. I might be new here, but I have plans that will make this school very interesting. The Queen has spoken and by the way. My name is Danielle Rose. Never forget it. It'll be bigger than any of the Dayton's." Her short speech is jaw dropping. The bell rings and they make their way to class.

"Hello class and welcome back, and to some of you that are new, welcome. This year we will be putting in a lot of work so keep the gossip and partying to a minimum." The British teacher introduced himself. "Now. I am Mr. English and I teach English. I was born and raised in England and moved here after college. Now everyone, go around and introduce yourselves." He adds. He was tall and slim and so sexy. His short red hair accented his blue eyes. He had a smile that invited you in with no question. "You, what's your name and where are you from?" He asks Danielle, now that it was her turn. "I am Danielle Rose. My family moved here from Savannah Georgia. My dad is buying The H. Hotel." Danielle answers. "It is very nice to have you here Ms. Rose." He smiles at her. His eyes were settled on her.

Unfortunately, the class came to an end and she was packing her things for algebra. "Ms. Rose. I look forward to having you here this year." He comments when everyone leaves the room. "I look forward to coming to your class every morning." She winks, exiting.

Lunch came, and Danielle sat at the table with her ladies. "What is this?" Danielle asks, as Amber sits the tray in front of Dani. "I got you your lunch. So you don't have to get up." She explained. "You don't have to do that, but thank you. Today is so overwhelming." Danielle starts eating the fries. "One for you, and one for you." A senior girl hands out a flyer. "Cheerleading? I think we should." Danielle sat the flyer down. "That would be so much fun." Amber smiles. "Not to mention it will look good on college applications." Crystal adds her two cents. "Sorry Crystal. Maybe next year, when you're not so... unqualified." The girl takes back the flyer. "You mean fat." Crystal puts her head down. "Hey, can I see these? Thanks." Danielle grabs the stack of flyers and throws them into the wind. At this point phones are out and ready. "Next time you think it's fun to bully someone, remember, I can be a bigger bully. Now get the hell away from this table." Danielle threatens. "This Queen stuff is all so new to me, you know." An obvious lie. "It'll take time, but you will get through it. You have us." Amber smiles at Dani. "You didn't have to do that." Crystal tries not to smile. "We are friends. No one comes between us. And no one hurts us."

Danielle squeezes their hands.

"What's up Ms. Queen of Oberlin?" Nate asks, mocking his sister. "I was doing just fine until you came over here. Now scram delinquent." She shoo's him away to his jock buddies. "He is so hot. Like a fire. You're so lucky to have him as a brother." Crystal fans herself off. "Ew. My brother is all but hot. I mean we have great genes, but ew. Get it together. You don't want to get mixed up with that. The only fire here is my love for firefighters and EMT'S. They lay down their lives every day to save lives, the least I can do is lay down." Danielle warns her. "Does he have like a dark past or something?" Crystal asks. Danielle shoots a look at her brother. "Or something." She answered. Little did she know. Mysterious was indeed alluring to Crystal.

Later that day. Danielle and her girls tried out for the junior cheer team. "What do we have here? Queen wannabe and her pack." The senior cheerleader comments. "We need fire for the junior team not an earthquake." The other girl at the table says. "Play this song. And it's password protected so don't try anything funny." Danielle flashed a smile. "You are so lucky that molly kicked in. I feel so fucking good right now." Crystal laughed. The girls posed, and the music started. Everything slowed down and Throughout the performance, the girls managed to stay in rhythm and Crystal managed to prove her dedication. Even when she started to sweat. "That was actually really good." One of the girls says, shocked. "Well, it was good. Definitely room for improvement." The senior captain fought the words but had to say them. "Looks like you three will be cheerleaders after all. I expect a workout plan for you though. Danielle can lead the junior squad." She directed it towards Crystal. "I won't disappoint." She replies. "I won't either." Danielle winks.

Carl, Lucas and Nate barged into the gym wearing short shorts and half cut T's. They cheered and mocked the cheerleaders in a playful way. "You nerds!" Danielle yelled, cracking up at the sight of her brother in short shorts. He ran over and spun her around. "Congrats." He laughs. "You must be her boo." The senior cheer captain pranced over to them. "Ew. God no. This is my twin brother." Danielle gagged. "Even better. Can't wait to see more of you." The senior cheer captain smiles.

2. A Star is born

Danielle was always one for dramatics, ever since she could remember. In elementary school, she met her best friend Brielle. They spent nearly everyday together. Shopping and people watching, some weekends they would stay locked away in Dani's room playing dress up and princesses. Danielle was always in control, but she would never take it too far to make Brielle upset.

In middle school, Brielle and Danielle formed their own clique called The Blossoms. It was a nod to redhead Blossom and her leadership skills in The Power Puff Girls. They were obsessed over and admired by many. Social media made them famous and they started gaining fame around Savannah. In eighth grade, they started getting invited to high school parties. "What about this?" Danielle asks, trying on a pearl tube top with a leather mini skirt. "Girl I love that!" Brielle was astonished, putting on lace cat ears.

Freshman and sophomore year, they dropped their clique and became inseparable. Half of the girls at the school desperately wanted to be their friends. The other half rolled their eyes and got upset when their boyfriends would drool over them. Then they became cheerleaders. "Since you girls basically run the school, Justin says you guys have to be at his party this weekend." Nate leaned over the kitchen island. "Party? That would be fun. Brielle, tell your mother that I love the remodeled home and I can't get it out of my head." Hazel smiles. "I will." Brielle returns the smile. "And I think we should go. I mean what's the worst that could happen? Nate is right, we are Queens." Brielle takes a bite of her cereal bar.

Saturday came, and Justin's party was in full effect. Kids from multiple schools were there and dancing like no one was watching. Weed was being grind, mixed and passed around. Danielle put her hair in a half top bun as the rest of the curls washed down her back. Her leather cami dress chokes her body tighter than the choker she wore. "Here. Tonight is going to be so fun." Danielle handed Brielle a blue pill that had what looks like a butterfly engraved in it. Butterflies were her favorite. "What is this?" Brielle asks as Danielle crushed it up and snorted it. Letting out a sigh of relief followed by the smile on her full red lips, Danielle looked at her. "It's molly. It's nothing bad I promise." She held out her pinky. The foundation of trust between them. Brielle swallowed it and took a sip of water. "If anything goes down find me ASAP. I will protect you two." Nate says, taking half of the last pill.

The night went on and...

Friday finally showed up and the girls had major plans.

"Tonight, is my sleep over. I know it sounds childish, but it'll be interesting, trust me. This will be a sleepover that you've never seen before." Danielle explains with a confident look on her face. "I can't wait. Honestly the girls are excited." Crystal clutches her books to her chest. "Nate." Danielle trots up to the jocks. "Tonight, you don't need to be there. Please find something to do." She begs. "I will be fine. I'll even stay in my room if you want." Nate contests. "Dude. We can find something to do." His new friend; Lucas butts in. "Please Lukey. Take him. Have fun you guys." She kisses Lucas on the cheek, leaving a red mark. "Anything for you Dani." Lucas smiles, gripping the black book bag straps. Danielle goes back to her friends. "Dude. Your sister is so hot. Like damn." He comments. "No. she's off limits." Nate shakes his head at the thought of them. "How about this? There is a frat party happening in the Villas. They will have the best-looking girls and the wildest games. It'll be fun. Tell your parents that you're staying at my house." Lucas plans. "Dude. Let's do it!" Nate gives him a bro hug.

The bell rang, and school was out. "I will see you ladies at my house at five sharp." Danielle walks down the hallway. "Ms Rose. A word." Mr. English waves her into his empty classroom. He closes the door behind her. "Your paper from Tuesday was great. Needs a little work though." He informed her. "What needs work if it was great?" She points out. She walks behind the desk for a better look. Her hand rests at the bottom of the page. His hand creeps to hers until it's sitting on top of hers. "I see. Maybe you can tutor me sometime." She looks into his eyes. "Well if you ever need some extra help with anything don't be afraid to ask for it." He says, writing his number on a neon yellow sticky note. "I will keep that in mind." Danielle slips it into her book as a teacher enters the room. "Hey, there is a meeting in the teachers' lounge." The woman informs. "Thank you. I will work harder. Pinky promise." Danielle leaves the classroom.

Only thirty minutes until Danielle's slumber party and everything was set up. Tiny beds placed around her room. Decorations and a chef for the girls. "Be safe tonight. No intense games like before Danielle." Felton says with a stern tone. "I understand daddy. We are simply going to just have fun and eat snacks and maybe watch movies or do each other's hair and makeup and just hang out." Danielle explains. "I mean it. Your mother and I are going on a well-deserved date night and we would like it to be undisturbed. Keep Nate away from the girls." Her father adds. "Nate get down here." He yells. Hazel enters the room wearing a royal blue dress with a gold zipper in the back and her blue heels. She clipped on her gold earrings. "Are you ready, my love?" She asks, kissing Felton's cheek. "Yes I am. You're so beautiful." He held her gently. She turned so he could zip her up.

Nate flew downstairs fully dressed. "Yeah dad?" He asks. "You have plans tonight?" Felton asks, surprised. "Yeah. I'm sleeping over Carl's house with some of the guys. I'm not being trapped in here with them." Nate explained zipping up his duffel bag. "Good, because none of us wanted you here." Danielle makes her way upstairs. "Be safe and have fun." Hazel kisses Nate as Lucas waits at the elevator. "We will go down with you. Dani behave!" Hazel yelled as they crowded the elevator.

Danielle sat at her vanity, twiddling the piece of paper between her fingers. Finally, she decided to do it. She texted him. *Hey. With a heart emoji.* Now she waits, but not for long. His reply was simple and sweet.

Him *<3: I thought you wouldn't text me.*

Dani*: I was getting ready for this sleepover with a few friends.* ~~*I just can't get you out of my head. Is that wrong?*~~

Him *<3: oh. Have fun. Going to have pillow fights and face masks? Lol.*

Dani*: Lol, no. We are just gossiping. Might go out on the town. Get into a little trouble.*

Him *<3: well I know a bar downtown that would be fun. It's called Harry's. I know it doesn't sound like a place you'd go but it's fun.*

Dani*: We will see how "fun" it is lol.*

Him *<3: Be careful. Wouldn't want anything happening to such a beautiful girl like yourself.*

Dani*: Hopefully a handsome man will be there to save me. Goodnight lover boy. Btw that's your new name in my phone <3 :)*

Loverboy*: I like it. My Queen. Goodnight.*

Five came and the girls arrived with their clothes. "Your place is so gorg! Totally worth sneaking out for." Trish comments, rushing in. "Thanks. I thought it was very homie. So, to start the night off I was thinking massages and then seaweed wrap and then facials." Danielle claps twice and the spa staff appear. "Yes. Yes. Yes!" Bethany runs to the table. "Trish, why did you have to sneak out?" Danielle asked. "My parents hate me that's why." Trish answers.

The clothes came off and the girls were now being massaged. "This feels absolutely amazing, especially after a long week." Amber groans. "This hot stone back massage is to die for." Danielle comments, checking out her freshly done claw nails. "A little lower please. Don't be shy." Trish tells the masseuse. "What are we doing after this?" Crystal asks through her facial mask. "Well maybe we can go to a bar. Get out of the rich and shiny life for a night. Who knows. Might even meet a bad boy." Danielle explains. "Oh, that actually sounds kind of fun, I am so down!" Amber yells.

"I have nothing to wear. Just these." Crystal shows off her collection of cute eighties themed clothes. "Cute but not acceptable. Come on." Danielle and the girls get ready to go to the city for a shopping spree. "I never had anyone to dress me before. And I'm fat no one would even look at me." Crystal looks at her lap. "You are not fat. You just have to feel confident in yourself to be a bad bitch and I am going to help build that confidence." Danielle pulled her head up. "What is your ideal weight?" Danielle asks. "Whatever Jason Mamoa weighs, that, on top of me." Crystal shoots back nearly snorting. Danielle rolled her eyes but couldn't help but laugh. Crystal pulled out her little red sponge and applied blush onto her chubby cheeks. "A sponge? What are you, an old church woman? No, we are going now!" Danielle pulled Crystal to the door. "It is hard looking for cute clothes for me. Fashion hates big girls." Crystal informs. "You just haven't given anything a chance." Danielle latches to Crystal's arm. "Before we go, can I use the bathroom really quick?" Crystal asked. "Yeah, through there." Danielle pointed the way.

The girls got dressed and played in make up while the sink water ran longer than it should have. Danielle knew exactly what was going on. Crystal exited. "Thought you were drowning yourself for a second." Danielle jokes. "I think lunch didn't settle right or something." Crystal laughs nervously. Danielle reached under her dresser for a bag of orange pills. "I used to do the same thing. This is a healthier way. They will make you not hungry, just do not take them at night. It's not fun." Danielle whispered. "What is it? Like crack?" Crystal whispered. "Wha- Crystal. It's Adderall. Jesus what kind of person do you take me for." Danielle was shocked. "I'm so sorry. Just nervous." Crystal covers her face.

The girls threw all the customers out of every store they went to. Danielle picked out all new outfits for Crystal. Dresses and skirts and tops of all kinds. The girls shut down Sephora and stocked up on new products. "You are not fat. You're thick. There's a difference. At least you're not a virgin." Danielle says to Crystal. "You aren't. Right?" Danielle asks, suspicions from the silence. "I've done other stuff. But I just never got that lucky." She responded, fixing her hair in the mirror. "She was the blow job Queen last year." Bethany laughed. "At least she could get it." Danielle snapped. "Lose it when you are ready. Not because you're pressured into it." Danielle assures her. "Or MAC lip gloss." Amber commented, holding the tube to her lips. Everyone just looked at her. "What? MAC lip gloss will always get you some dick. So I have heard." Amber says. Crystal picks up two.

The clock struck nine thirty, and the girls changed and were ready to head out. Danielle wore a short dress. Half was solid blue and the other half was made like a leather biker jacket with thigh high boots. Her fire orange hair curled down her sides. She led the pack to Harry's Bar. "This is a cute little bar, but how are we going to drink?" Bethany asks. "Hun, you use these. Those will make guys do anything." Danielle grabs Amber's boobs.

When they walked in the bar, classic rock music blared, and people were smoking and drinking beer. Some guys crowded the pool tables. One guy was at the bar. Familiar backside. Deep blue eyes hidden under a black ball cap. "Go have fun." Danielle walks over to a pool table. A group of young guys checking her out. "You seem to be in the wrong place, pretty lady." One says. "I like to have some fun once in a while. Be adventurous. How about you show me how you guys play, Because where I'm from, I'd whoop that ass." Danielle flirts. "Rack em up Bobby." He yells, putting the toothpick in the corner of his mouth. "Can I have your name?" He asks. "Win and I'll give it to you." She grabs a pool stick. The man at the bar watches quietly. She spots and winks. The girls spread around the bar dancing and mingling. Crystal snags a cute one and they go outside to smoke.

"So, are you from around here?" He asks, lighting a cigarette. "No. From the Hampton area." Crystal pulls out a lollipop and starts to suck on it. "So, what is a girl like you doing down here talking to a guy like me?" He asks. "Being adventurous. Having a little fun. I don't even know your name though." Crystal smiles. "Does it matter?" He says, pulling out a condom. "You're so fucking hot. And if I can't see you when I want to, then let me give you a reason to come back." He whispers, his hands start to move higher up her skirt. His lips press against hers as she leads him behind the bar. Pushing him against the wall, Crystal was on her knees. He begs her to stop. "What's wrong?" Crystal asks, looking up at him like a puppy. "That's the best head I've ever had. Let me show you what I can do." He lets out a nervous laugh. Crystal is against the wall, a leg on his shoulder. His tongue danced on her skin, twirled gently as she covered her mouth to not make a noise. He stood up and put the condom on. He kissed her neck as he entered her slowly. She couldn't handle being quiet anymore. She looked up at the stars. It felt good. It felt greater than she could have imagined, and then he was finished. He tossed the condom aside and gave her his number. "That was really great. See you around." She says, biting her lip. "I'm Vic. Wait, how old are you?" He asked in a laugh. "If I told you, you'd freak out. Vic." She blew a kiss and entered the bar.

Nate and Carl became close quickly. They mostly liked the same thing. Football, parties and girls. It was almost as if they were the same person. They both made long mental lists of the things they liked and disliked about females.

They liked short skirts and short shorts, they also liked flats and heels of all kinds. But not flip flops or slides unless they are only worn in the house only. Carl mostly liked tan lines, long necks, long hair to pull on. Good posture and fruity perfume. Girly girls were his go to. He liked full lips, and small noses. Light makeup, but not too much that made you look like a clown. Nate liked laid back girls. Girls that aren't afraid to get dirty and have fun. He hated snobby girls and girls who were too good for certain activities. I guess you could say his sister, but even she likes to keep people on their toes.

At the frat party, Nate dances and mixed into the crowd. The music exploded through the windows. There were multiple joints being passed around. Carl did a line of coke and headed upstairs with some girl. "Bro you want some?" A man, obviously not a high schooler asks. "What are they?" Nate investigates the tiny bag that held two pills inside. "MDMA" The man says. "Molly. It's safe and good. I usually sell them at seventy-five, but since you're new I'll do fifty as a first-time customer. I'll even throw in a free one." He convinces. "You should be a car salesman. Here, a hundred. I don't knock anyone's hustle bro." Nate slaps the bill into his hand. "Thanks bro. The name is Dallas." He says. "Nate." They shook hands again. "If you ever need anything, you know where to find me." Dallas says.

Sneaking out a joint of his own, Nate sat on the dock drinking his beer and thinking. "Hey, get out of here." This guy yells, slurring his words. "I don't want any trouble bro." Nate held his hands up in surrender. "I know you. I heard rumors about you. You a bitch." The guy stepped closer. "Get out of my face." Nate stood his ground. The wind calmed down. The music started to fade from the anger. He whispered one word to him, and that was the feather that broke the camel's back. Nate punched and punched and kicked and slammed and got lost in the anger. Everything was red. The guy. His face. Nathaniel's hands. And then he stood up. Taking everything in. The motionless body on the grass.

3. Brotherhood

When Nate was young he always had someone to look up to. His dad was the best businessman he knew, given he was a child at the time. His older brother Donovan was popular, handsome and friendly. Everyone loved him. Sometimes Nate thought his father favored him more. Donovan and Danielle could get away with murder, but not Nate. In reality, Felton always only wanted the best for his kids. He was secretly in competition with his childhood best friend Julian Dayton.

In middle school, things started changing. Donovan was in his last years of high school, Danielle became a party girl with her best friend Brielle. Nate sometimes hated to admit it, but he had a small crush on Brielle. Now it wasn't because she was black or unattractive. She was beautiful. He just spends so much time with her growing up he saw her as a sister. Was it wrong to have these feelings?

Nate developed anger issues that grew worse and worse. There wasn't anything he could really pinpoint it to. His father was always working, and his mother was nice, but she never showed the public that she had a back bone. Until that night. Nate was drunk, he was threatening him. He had no choice but to fight him he thought. So, he did.

Freaking out, Nate paced back and forth. "What did I do? What did I do? Fuck!" He runs his hands through his orange hair. "Nate!" Lucas ran down to the dock. "Woah. What happened?" Lucas asked. "I didn't mean to. I... I..." Nate couldn't find the words. "Stay here!" Lucas ran into the party.

Moments later, Lucas returned to the dock with some of the team. "Rose, get in the water. Wash off and then wait in my truck. Go around the house and do not be seen by anyone. Don't touch anything with your hands. Boys. Get me the tarp from the shed and use your shirt as gloves. Roll him under the dock." Carl orders. He took the initiative and hid the body. "Let's go. Now." Carl casually gets into his truck and they take off back to his house.

Nathaniel, now traumatized, sat on the floor staring into space. "Take a shower." Lucas tossed a towel at him.

Turning on the waterfall shower, Nate stood there and cried to himself. This was supposed to be his new start. His family's new start. He let his anger take control. He'd killed a man. He'd killed a man. He'd killed a man. He tried to breathe through the thoughts, but it kept getting worse and worse.

The eight-ball rolled into the pocket. "You are really good. Maybe we should have bet on something else." The guy stated. "Maybe you should be better at betting." Danielle winks, gloating. "Alright. Alright. My name is Sanford, but my friends call me Dice." He smiles. "I hope that's because they are being cute. Because you're not lucky." Danielle laughs. The other girls are flirting and drinking and dancing all around still. "Be right back." She steps away.

Danielle steps into the bathroom to fix herself in the mirror. Pool stick guy strutted in. "Unlucky and illiterate. This is a women's bathroom." Danielle says. "Oh please. Don't think you weren't teasing and not going to get anything." Pool Stick guy grabbed her hips. "Get off of me." Danielle yelled, trying to push him off. "Shut up!" Pool Stick guy pinned her against the wall. His hand over her mouth. Her dress started lifting. And then the door broke open. George rushed in and pulled Pool Stick guy off her. "Get off of her." He yelled. Danielle ran out of the bathroom and clung on to the pool table. She witnessed George pull Pool Stick guy out of the room and beat him up. She ran over to them and pulled him off. "You need to get out of here." She orders. George stood up, ran to his car and sped off into the night.

Danielle gathered the girls and headed back to the car. "What's wrong? What was that?" Crystal asked. "I just want to go home. It's getting late. I wanted no part of that drama." Danielle flipped her hair. The car headed back to the H where Danielle knew she would be safe. "You literally had two guys fighting over you!" Crystal says with excitement. "That was terrifying. He followed me into the bathroom." Danielle shut her down. "People just really need to chill the fuck out. We are all on this floating rock and can't escape. Why can't they go do something productive?" Danielle added.

When they arrived back to the apartment, Danielle went straight to her bed and hid under the covers. The girls all crawled into their beds and went to sleep peacefully. One little tear slid down the cheek of Danielle's face. As she silently cried. Now she knew what she went through.

Nate sat at the edge of the bed still thinking about the man in the tarp. "Listen to me. We are a brotherhood. We stick together no matter what. As captain of this team, I will make sure anything that will ruin this team gets taken care of quickly." Carl says, sipping his bud light. "Coach didn't pick you." Lucas commented. "No, but Natey boy over there will make sure he does." Carl smiles at the team. "A simple price for the favor I just did." Carl adds on. "It's only a favor, if I asked you to help me. I didn't ask for this. I didn't ask for any of this!" Nate exclaimed. "You represent our team when you are in and out of that fucking jersey. We as a team will always help each other out no matter what. If that's too much for you." Carl lowers his tone and holds Nate against the wall. "Then get off of my fucking team. Your choice." He throws Nate down.

Nate looks at the other players for back up. Silence filled the room. None of them would be on his side, not with this. Then he forced out a sigh. "Fine." Nate gave up his alpha role.

Felton and Hazel returned home to the quiet apartment. Checking on the sleeping girls. Relieved that the apartment wasn't a wreck. "Maybe moving here wasn't a mistake after all." Hazel smiles. Walking over to Danielle and kissing her forehead. "I told you. We don't have to worry about them. They are taking it easy. They are staying out of trouble and most importantly they are safe." Felton hugged his wife. "We raised them right. Even with everything that happened." Hazel started spinning Felton in her arms. Slowly dancing. No music, just love.

Danielle is woken up by her buzzing phone in the middle of the night. "**Lobby.**" She reads. Putting on her pj's, Danielle makes her way to the elevator. "Where are you sneaking off to?" Hazel asks. "Lobby real quick." Danielle tucks a piece of her hair behind her ear. "Okay. Hurry back up." Hazel stood in the kitchen, pouring her Moscato.

The elevator doors opened and there he stood. His eyes lit up. She stepped out of the elevator as he rushed up to her. George held her in his arms and kissed life back into her. "I couldn't get you out of my head. Are you okay?" His accent was strong. "I couldn't either. I am fine. Thank you for saving me." Danielle smiles. She pulls him into the outside patio. They sit, kissing on a bench. "I will always be there for you. I think I am in love with you. If I have to keep this quiet or leave the school I will." He confesses. "I can't let you do that. Teaching is what you've always wanted to do. But if keeping quiet will be better. It won't be forever." She whispered back. "I have to go now. I will see you on Monday." Danielle gives him one last kiss and heads back to her home.

Tip toeing through her room trying not to wake the girls, Danielle sees Bethany covering herself quickly as if she didn't want to get caught. Danielle gets back in her bed and sleeps as if nothing was wrong. All wrong.

The New York sunlight entered the windows of the Rose fortress. The girls sat around the table eating the beautiful breakfast the chef made up. "Did everyone have fun last night?" Hazel asks, chewing her food. "Yeah we had fun. Maybe we will do it again sometime." Danielle answers. "So, tell me about your night." Felton pushed the conversation. "Oh, well we had massages and did each other's make up and just hung out around the town. That's all." Danielle kept out a few parts. Nate stormed in and went to his room without a word. "I think I left my phone in your room. I will be back." Crystal says, leaving the table.

Three unanswered knocks, Crystal decided to barge in. "If I didn't say come in it means don't come in." Nate yelled. "Oh. Sorry. I think you have the wrong room." He added, finally turned around seeing Crystal. "I think you just need to destress. You're so... tense." She creeps over to him, caressing his arm. "No thanks. I'm not interested." He pushed her arm off of him. "What? Are you gay or something?" She asked. "I don't want you. I get it, fat girls are good at sex because that's all they can get. But I'm not interested." He says walking past her to open the door. She grabs his arm causing him to push her out of his room and onto the ground.

Crystal gathered her things and started to leave. "Girls. My ride's here. See you at school." Crystal lied, and Danielle knew it. "See you at school." Danielle flashes a smile. "Someone got rejected."

Bethany laughs. "Gosh Beth. They did such a great job. No one should ever know." Danielle commenter. "Know what?" Bethany snapped at her. "That you're a dude." Danielle laughs with the rest of the girls. Bethany threw her fork down and stormed out of the apartment.

Dani: *I know we are great friends, but stay away from my brother.*

Crys: *I have no idea what you're talking about. See you Monday. Lol. Kisses****

Nate makes his way downstairs and makes a plate of food. "Nice of you to join us. I thought you were sleeping over." Felton greets. "Just had a long night. And I did, just came home early." He answers in a low tone. "Well, what did you do?" Hazel asks, sipping her coffee. "We just hung out. Nothing special." Nate suddenly was distracted by something on his phone. "I gotta meet someone. Be back soon." He leaps up and runs to the elevator. "I'm officially worried." Hazel keeps eating. Felton places his hand on hers. "He is fine." He whispers.

Nate exits the elevator on the rooftop to find Erica looking over the edge at the city. "Don't jump." Nate laughs. "My father jumped off of a building and died you asshole!" She yells. "Oh god. I'm so sorry. I didn't mean it!" He started to panic. That angry expression started to turn into a laugh. "I'm totally kidding." Erica bursts out in a laugh. "You're an ass." Nate joins in on the laughing. "I had to. So where did you disappear to last night?" She asks. "I was hanging out with the team and... well we just played games and passed out." Nate lied. "Oh. That's cool. I was just home, writing." She lets out a sigh.

There was an awkward silence between the two as Nate leaned over the railing. He noticed her pulling her red long sleeves over her hands as if she was hiding something. "So, you write?" He asks. "Yeah. Ever since my sister died, I was told that writing would be a great outlet. Even on my school's newspaper committee." She rolled her eyes. "That isn't bad. My father has a plan for all of his kids. My brother is to become the world's best lawyer, me a star pro-football player, and my sister a businesswoman. So, moving here, to the state of endless opportunity has enhanced his views." Nate lets out a slight laugh while Erica studied his face. "You don't want that?" She catches his eye. "As of lately, I think I want to go a different route in life, but I am stuck." He looks down at his hands. Seeing the blood on them. He starts to tremble. Erica hesitantly grabbed his hand, snapping him out of the horror. "It will be okay. I am here now." Erica moves closer, inviting Nate in. Their breathing started to match speed. Their lips almost touch and then...

"Ew! So, this is what you are doing up here all the time. Or should I say who you're doing." Danielle approached slowly. "Dani, go away!" Nate ordered her to leave. "No. I need to talk to you." She refused. Then looking at Erica, judging her clothes. "Alone trollop!" She demanded. Erica rolls her eyes and walks to the other side of the roof. "What did you do to Crystal?" Danielle folded her arms. The August wind blew her orange hair, strands covering her face, getting stuck in her lip gloss. "Nothing. Your little whore friend tried kissing me and I pushed her away." Nate told the truth. "That better be all. Stay away from my friends. By the way, dad told me to let you know there's a dinner party Friday so be there and sober." Danielle stormed inside.

Erica approached him hesitantly. "What was that about?" She asks. "My sister's friend tried to kiss this morning and I pushed her away and she ran home." Nate explains honestly. "Well, I mean who wouldn't be compelled to kiss you you're..." Erica trailed off. "I am what?" A smirk grew on his face. "You are... Handsome." She rolled her eyes. "And you are beautiful, so now what?" He quickly responds. Erica looks up at him with a warming smile. Then she looks down at her buzzing phone. "I am being summoned home. Same time tomorrow?" Erica yells, skipping to the door. "You got it." Nate smiles. He walks over to the edge. Rubbing his foot over a burn mark on the floor.

Nate and Erica spent a lot of time together over the next few days. She would show up at his practices and they even moved from their normal spot to hanging out around the city. She sits on the bleachers of Oberlin's football field. The cheerleader's practices on the fake grass. Danielle sways over to Erica in a white tank top and black short shorts. "You know, I have seen you around my brother a lot. You guys dating?" Danielle asks, fixing her half up ponytail. "Something like that." Erica laughs. "Well, just be careful. He is a jock. Jocks are messy." She plants a seed into her ear. "He's not that kind of person. He is sweet and gentle." Erica argues. "Hun, I am his twin. I know him inside and out. What athletes do you know that's gentle, honest and loyal? Name one and I will go away." Danielle challenges. "Stephen Curry." Erica named with a confident smile. "Well played. I will go." Danielle stands up. The football flew through the air and hit the cart of a ROTC guy. He dropped all of the equipment and angrily threw the ball back. The cheerleaders and football players laughed. Danielle saw an opportunity. She trotted over to him and helped him. "I am sorry for them. They are jerks." She says in a soft tone. "Yeah they are." He hasn't looked up yet. "Very randomly, someone amazing comes into your life, and here I am." Danielle touched his hand. He looks up at her and their eyes catch for the first time. "I am Jason. Jason Merrit." He stumbles over his words. He had short blonde hair and blue eyes that reminded her of the Savannah River. "I'm Danielle." She smiles that smile she flashes to solidify what she wants. "I.. I know." He smiles back, blushing. They both stand and she hands him the equipment. "I have to get back. See you around." She flirts, caressing his arm.

The team finished their practice and gathered in the locker room. "You guys have been doing a great job out there these past few weeks. I have been observing each and every one of you. I personally think Mr.Terril will lead this team great. You all are brothers. Stick together, look out for each other. You have an iron will, drive, determination, keep that, hold it with everything you got! Others will see what I see, and they'll try to take it. It will lead you to greatness. On three! OBL!" Coach makes his announcement. "Knights!" The team yelled and cheered and jumped in the air. "OBL!" The coach repeats. "Knights!" Lucas gave a look to Nate. He knew something wasn't right. Nate gathered his things and left the locker room.

"Stop being a hoe." Crystal comments. "What do you mean? I am just being nice." Danielle laughed. Suddenly looking over and seeing George watching. "Why does he always watch our practices?" Bethany comments. "It's creepy." She adds. "Maybe he is watching the football team." Danielle says, packing her stuff up. "Like clockwork." Bethany whispers as the other ladies leave. "What the hell did you just say to me?" Danielle stepped closer to her. "Every time someone says something you're there to his defense. You think I didn't see what happened in that garden at your sleepover? I believe the word is leverage. You don't scare me Danielle." Bethany shoulder checked her.

"Underestimate me so I can embarrass you." Danielle hissed, shooting a look at George who was now walking to his car. She knew she had to do it. Something she really didn't want to do. "Amber, Crystal. Meet me in the drama room asap!" Danielle ordered.

Sitting alone on the edge of the stage, she thinks about her next move. "What happened?" Crystal hurried in. "Yeah, why the SOS?" Amber drops her duffel back. "As Queen, I need something to make me powerful. Where I come from, secrets hold power. Bitchany saw me making out with a guy at the bar and decided she was going to tell people it was Mr. English. As much as I would love to just devour his face before sitting on it, I need to put an end to that rumor before it even starts. That would ruin his life and spoil my name." Danielle chose her words carefully. "Then we will get you secrets and give her hell." Crystal looks at Amber. "Let's take this bitch down." Amber smiles. "We will teach her not to mess with us. What should we call ourselves, ladies?" Danielle flashed a devious smile. "We don't need a name to show our strength." Amber commented. "My mother always told me to put things back where I found them. So let's put this bitch in her place." Danielle admires herself in the drama room mirror. "You girls are invited to tomorrow's dinner party by the way. Please save me from my misery. I still haven't found someone to wear." Danielle sighed. "Let's go shopping today. Nails and dresses." Amber says with excitement. "Oh yes!" Crystal smiles. "It'll be a good excuse to get out of the house. I really need it." Amber pulled Danielle up and towards the door.

The girls stopped by the nail salon and did as girls do in the salon, gossip. "This pink. With metallic rose gold middle finger." Danielle chose her colors. "Oh claws. Love them." Crystal complimented. "Yellow, but this one I want daisies on them. Thank you." Crystal added. "This one and this finger plaid." Amber put her hands on the towel. "So why did you freak out when I asked to go to your house?" Danielle whispered. "What are you talking about?" Amber laughed it off. "Honey. I am far from stupid. You spazzed like you were on an episode of Cops." Danielle raised an eyebrow. "Things aren't the best at home. Mom and dad pretty much hate each other. That's all." Amber looked down at her nails. "I am so sorry. I understand completely." Danielle let it go. "By the way. Totally scored some hot tea." Amber gloated. "Spill!" Crystal gasped. "So you know Gio is like the most liked homophobe in school. Well a birdie told me that he has been hooking up with Gio for years." Amber smiled. "How is that tea? I don't know who Gio is. "Well, the guy who told me was Aaron and Aaron is best friends with Jenny who is Gio's sister." Amber finished. "Didn't Aaron catfish people? So I've heard." Danielle asked. "He was set up but you know people. Once they have a face to the rumor it's over for you. He lost so many friends I feel bad for him. But that's life." Amber replied.

Friday night guests started to arrive at the penthouse. Everyone dressed in beautiful gowns and suits. Danielle sat at her vanity dressed in her pink Sherri Hill gown. She looked like a princess. "I feel like we are underdressed." Amber laughs, sipping her drink. Amber sat on the bed in her yellow sancta Sophia dress as if someone was painting her. "Or Danielle is just dramatic." Crystal laughed. "Why isn't Trish here?" Danielle asked, fixing her hair. "She had some date tonight, I think." Crystal answered, taking selfies. "A date is more important than a dinner party with friends?" Danielle rolled her eyes. "We have to go to this party tomorrow night." Crystal says, taking a puff from her juul. "We should!" Danielle finishes her makeup. "Bitch you're gonna die." Amber says. "Bitch let me die." Crystal laughed back. "Princess Dani, the guests are waiting." Nate knocked on the door.

The kids joined the guests in the penthouse dinner party. Conversations of all kinds floated around the room. The waiters swayed around to hand out drinks and finger food. "They really went all out for this. I love it." Amber complimented. "Oh please, my father is just kissing ass." Nate shot his drink back. "Nathaniel, come I would like you to meet someone." Felton smiled.

"This is Marshall Dudley. He is on the board of The H." Felton introduced. "Nice to meet you Mr. Dudley." Nate had a firm handshake. "The grip of a football star. I can't wait to see what you can do on the field." He comments. "Father. How are you?" Donovan entered the room with Elizabeth on his arm. "Always lovely to see you." Elizabeth hugs Felton. "I am going to find Hazel." She excused herself. "We are discussing the business deal of the century." Felton fills Donovan in. "The board is all on the same page. We looked into your handling of your other hotels and I think this will be a good move for the future." Marshall patted Felton's shoulder.

"I figured you'd be in here." Elizabeth entered the side room. "Leave us." Elizabeth ordered the man. She sat in his seat and sipped her wine. "You know he shouldn't have been in here with you alone. What would Felton think?" Elizabeth brushed off her Marchesa Gown. "Donovan did it to you didn't he?" Hazel scooted over. "I don't know what you're talking about." Elizabeth rolled her eyes. "Ah, the denial. I know my family. I know my son. He has a wandering eye. And that is okay." Hazel snickers to herself. "You think I am doing this alone? Felton has had his hand full of confidants over the years. Lawyers, real estate agents, business partners, you name it. You must want to fight. Take the power. Let those women know who you are. It wasn't that I never liked you. I knew you were weak. You wouldn't be able to handle my son or our name. But now you have the name. Show them what a Rose is capable of." Hazel exited the room.

"So, you are like the Beckham family." Amber comments, staring at Donovan. "Literally, everyone in your family is attractive." Crystal adds. "That is so not true, I have a cousin that looks like Carl from Jimmy Neutron." Danielle laughs, Amber nearly spat out her drink. "That isn't funny Dani. Leave him alone." Donovan walks over to the group. "Not everyone is going to think I am funny or pretty and that is okay. They are wrong though." Danielle flips her hair behind her. "How have you been?" Donovan laughs, hugging her. "I am settling in. These are my friends. Amber and Crystal." Danielle introduces. "They think you're hot." Danielle adds, embarrassing them. "What- no, I am Crystal." Crystal stutters over her words. "Nice to meet you ladies. Enjoy your night." Donovan smiles. "You are an ass." Amber busts out on a laugh.

"Hazel, how do you feel about making a debut as The Hampton's new uprising family?" The reporter asked. "This is all new to us, but we will carry the title gracefully. The Dayton's left some big shoes to fill, but we will fill them. Enjoy the party." Hazel answers.

The dinner party was coming to an end, and Felton stood on the bottom stair. "I want to thank everyone who showed up tonight. We are not only here to introduce us as the new family in the neighborhood. But to build relationships and to get to know you all. I am in talks to buy The H and make it great again." Felton started. The family joined him for the press pictures. "This will be the start of a new era. A breath of fresh air. To a new start." Felton held up his glass as everyone else followed. "A new start is right." Danielle winked at Nate. "Stop it." Hazel whispered.

The guests left and the help started to clean the home. "Thank you both for behaving tonight. It means a lot." Felton kissed Danielle on the forehead and hugged Donovan and Nate. "We always behave." Danielle smiles.

Saturday came and word around school was that a popular bad boy was throwing a house party. Dallas' house was beautiful and big. The girls packed inside Amber's SUV. "Alright bitches, sluts and whores. Let's get lit!" Amber yelled with excitement. Crystal pulled out her weed vape pen and passed it around. Clouds of smoke filled the car. Music blared inside. The car stopped at the corner. A girl holding a sparkly bookbag. Trish. "What the hell?" Danielle asked. "My mom is like super against hanging out and parties. Sneaking out feels rebellious." Trish answered. By ten o'clock, everyone was arriving.

By midnight, the music was vibrating the trees, people in the pool and smoking, dancing with the people inside and outside. Black light made colors glow all over. Danielle and her girls showed up like models. The guys checked them out. The girls either admired them or rolled their eyes. Crystal fixed her orange glowing eyeliner and glitter covered eyelids. Nate and Lucas stood in the kitchen. Nate being Lucas' wingman for these girls that were from a school in the Upper East Side. Sarah and Nate shared a joint and danced together. Danielle and Crystal spotted a guy standing on the wall in a colorful striped shirt. "Make it less obvious." Danielle approached him. "What? I am just selling smarties." He says holding them up. "Gross." Danielle replied. "We will take two. She's new to this area." Crystal laughs. "Forty." He says, checking Danielle out. The girl's each pulled a twenty dollar bill out of their bra's and handed it over. "Thank you." They synced, taking the molly from him. "I'm Dallas." He smiles. "Danielle." She winked.

The two went into the bathroom and they swallowed the pills. "To a night of being bad bitches." Danielle freshens up in the mirror. "To the start of the school year of being those bitches." Crystal touches up her red full lips. "Have you ever done acid?" Crystal asked. "I'm not big on psychedelics. But I bet that Dallas guy knows. And don't sleep with him like Bethany is sleeping with that girl she was posted up with in the corner." Danielle comments. "I love how colorful you wear your makeup. Bold, euphoric and bomb aesthetic. Love it. Never change. Let's go." Danielle opened the door.

Lucas lit his newly wrapped joint, but before he could take a hit Danielle snatched it and took a deep inhale. "Whoa! Careful Queen. You can't handle it." Lucas laughed. Jumping on to the counter, Danielle exhaled the smoke into the air. "I can handle a lot more than you think." Danielle winks. "Go away." She turns to the girls and orders. "Luc. That's my sister bro." Nate says. "Oh, now you care? Sarah, take him." Danielle snaps, handing Sarah the joint. "That's mine." Lucas reaches for it. Danielle takes another hit and pulls Lucas to her. Her lips touch his and she blows it into his mouth. Her tongue licking his bottom lip. "Sarah, you can have it." Lucas bites his lip, staring deep into Dani's eyes. "Dance with me." Danielle pulls him to the dance floor. "I can't dance." He laughs. "I don't remember asking if you could." Danielle pulls him close to her. Both grinding against each other. The music devouring them. Lucas built the courage after weeks of crushing on Danielle to kiss her. So, he did. She pulled him closer and bit his lip. Surprised, he looked into her eyes. He wanted her. He craved her. She took his hand and led him upstairs to the bedroom. Pushing him on the bed, Danielle kissed him and kissed his neck. His hands explored her body and then slid up her dress. "You have to earn that." She whispered, nibbling at his ear. "How do I earn it?" Lucas asks. "I guess we will see." Danielle winks, exiting the room.

Amber was outside dancing and socializing about outfits and boys and refused drinks from everyone trying to hand her one. "Come on, it's a party." A guy says. "Drinking is just not my thing." Amber refuses. "You're no fun." He laughs. "Come swimming with me, since I'm no fun." Amber walks over to the pool. "What?" He asks as she slides off her dress and crawls into the warm pool. He follows her lead. Now in his boxers, he swims to her and kisses her. "You are crazy." He whispers. "And what does that make you?" She smiles, kissing him back. "What are you doing?" Trish asks. "Swimming." Amber laughs. "My mom called your mom. I have to go. Now." Trish panicked. Amber rushed out of the pool and got dried off. "Where is Crys?" Amber asks. "I haven't seen her or Dani. Let's go!" Trish pushed through the party with her stuff in her hands.

Amber*: I am taking Trish home. She is in trouble. If you guys need to be picked up please text me!*

Crystal sat in a room that was lit up in blue and red lights, just her and Carl. "So, what do you want from me?" She asked, leaning back on the bed. "We all know. You're a big girl. We all know big girls will do anything for a little attention. So come here and suck this dick." Carl walked up to her and pulled out his dick. It was bigger than she thought it would be, given his ego. "You first." She pulls her dress up and lays back. "Yes ma'am. And don't say a word to anyone." He puts his beer down and gets on his knees. What she didn't realize, the phone camera aiming at them from the dresser.

"Mom?" Trish called out. "This is what we do now? Lie? I told you about hanging around them. What if someone from the church saw you?" Mrs. Sampson yelled. "No one would have. They are my friend's mom. I want to live a normal life for once." Trish yelled back. Mr. Sampson entered the room as Mrs. Sampson slapped her. Her father pulled her mother back to stop her from anything else happening. "Go to your room and pray for forgiveness for whatever other sins you committed tonight." She ordered.

4.Your Majesty

Crystal was always a happy kid, she was handed everything she wanted. Her mother and father shared the perfect marriage, they never fought, not in front of Crystal. They never mistreated her or hurt her like the kids at school did. Crystal wasn't the girl you'd see on the posters or commercials. She always has been on the larger side. No one ever wrote her love letters or gave her those romantic looks. They all saw her as the funny fat girl. Except one guy. Every year, her father's best friend's family came and spent a few weeks with them. Their son, Ramon was eighteen and just graduated high school when Crystal was thirteen. Crystal and Ramon spent nearly every second together. He taught her how to play XBox, she was nearly a beast on GTA online. They watched movies and went to the beach and then one night he walked into her room and cuddled up to her. "I can't sleep." He whispers. "You can stay here." She replied. She liked the way he made her feel. He kept scooting closer and closer. She knew it was wrong. She knew what he would do. And when it was over, she knew she would have to keep it quiet forever. After that, he vanished. Never to be seen again. Not by her, anyways.

Mrs. Radcliffe sits outside of the women's prison in

Atlanta Georgia. After two years inside and no probation and early release for good behavior. Looks like money really can buy anything. Bryanna walks out of the prison gates and hugs Mrs. Radcliffe tight. "You have no idea how much I have missed you." Bryanna smiles. "I am so happy you are out. And you did the right thing by turning yourself in. I am so proud of you." Mrs. Radcliffe opens the passenger door to the limo.

"So, where is she? How is she doing? I miss her so much." Bryanna threw out questions like a dodgeball game in elementary school. "She is absolutely beautiful and sweet and a cheerful little thing." Mrs. Radcliffe smiles at the description of her granddaughter. Bryanna looks down at her hands. "I am really glad you are home." She adds. "I am too. Just wish things were…" Bryanna trailed off at the thought. Her sisters, parents and husband were all dead. She was all alone. With nothing. "You have me and Chanel. We will look after you for as long as you need." Mrs. Radcliffe pulled her head on her shoulder.

The limo arrives at the mansion. She looks up and the memory of the first time she was brought there. She was so nervous to be out of New York for the first time without her sisters or parents. With the guy she knew she was going to love. *"My mother should be inside." Grayson smiles at her. His smile gave her a sense of calm. He pulled her up the stairs by her hand like you see in those couples' pictures. The two kids run inside and the butler; Mason smiles and asks her name. "I am sure you will absolutely love it here." He says in a typical*

British accent. "Thank you." She says bowing a little. They all laugh. "Oh sweetheart, how I've missed you." Mrs. Radcliffe hurries up to Grayson and hugs him. "And who is this lovely young woman?" His father asks. "I am Bryanna. Bryanna Dayton." She smiles, shaking his hand.

Bryanna shakes out of the memory when she sees her daughter. "Hey my love." She smiles, bouncing her in her arms. "Do you remember me?" She smiles. Chanel is shy at first, gets a familiar feeling and hugs Bryanna tight. "Alright, it is lunchtime." Mrs. Radcliffe picks up Chanel and puts her in the pink highchair. Mason brings her some food in a fancy dish. "I will show you to your room." Mrs. Radcliffe escorts Bryanna to her new room. "Now my room is on the west wing as you may know. If you need anything, please do not hesitate." She explains, opening the door. "Thank you. You don't know how much this means to me." Bryanna gives her one last hug before turning in for the night. "You are family. Nothing will change that. Goodnight Bryanna. See you bright and early." She walks away.

Bryanna enters the room and plops on the soft bed. The white sheets hide her away from the world. And in an instant, Bryanna is asleep.

Morning invites the sun rays into the room as Bryanna awakens. She lay in the white clawfoot tub and relaxed. This was her first actual bath away from other women and quick showers, barely washing. She ducks beneath the water and washed her wavy, long brown hair. She was refreshed and ready to take on the day. Three small knocks appeared at the bathroom door, causing her to nearly jump out of her skin. "Mrs. Radcliffe, breakfast is ready." Mason informed. "Thank you. I will be down." Bryanna yells, getting out and drying off. She takes a moment to cherish the ring Grayson slid on her finger. "I miss you so much." She whispers.

In the room was a set of new clothes. Jeans and a yellow tank top. Putting her hair in a messy bun and dressing, she skipped down to the dining room to find Chanel and Mrs. Radcliffe eating. The room smells like baked pastries and fruit. Like her home used to every morning. *"Morning Car." Bryanna greeted, pouring her orange juice. "Morning Bry." Carissa answered with her mouth full.*

"Ew! That's not attractive. And that much food will make you fat." Annabella whispered, making a parfait from the yogurt and fresh fruit Ramon laid out for her. "You know me so well." She thanked him. "Only the best for Miss. Dayton." He smiles. "Shut up! Car, you look just fine! Let's go." Bryanna grabbed her car keys. Something in the newspaper caught her attention. "Anna, you look like a call girl in that photo." Bryanna commented. "Better than a smelly jock." Annabella winked. "Oh, isn't that what you like?" Bryanna raised an eyebrow. "Good morning." Mrs. Radcliffe smiles. "You weren't kidding about bright and early." Bryanna comments, kissing and playing with Chanel before making her plate. "Always. Can't sleep forever. No matter how tempting it is." She answers. "Where is Mr. Radcliffe?" Bryanna asks. "He is in New York. With everything that happened, we decided to get a divorce. He wanted to forget and move on and that is something a mother cannot do easily." She explains. "I am so sorry. Well you are a strong woman. I know you will be happy soon if not already." Bryanna assures her. She takes a bite of her waffles. Two years of having prison food. She definitely took the Upper-Class lifestyle for granted. Before she knew it, Bryanna scarfed down her breakfast. "That good huh?" Mrs. Radcliffe laughs. "You have no idea." Bryanna was embarrassed. "I had to be strong. Especially after the video your sister put out." Mrs. Radcliffe. "She was always one for the dramatics. She had a simple plan

and it failed." Bryanna's smirk started to disappear. "It just doesn't make sense. Three bodies and her? I didn't even get to ask any questions." Bryanna comments, sipping her morning coffee. "I know. But now you are free, and you can take care of your family." Mrs. Radcliffe finishes her coffee and exits the room.

"Looks like it's just you and I pumpkin." Bryanna gently pinched Chanel's cheek. Then it hit her. This is the life she will have. Leaving everything she's ever known behind. She ran from her life to protect the last person she loves.

Bryanna ambled into the living room, past a familiar face. Chanel latched on to her hip. Two men. Very opposite from each other stood in the living room. "Uncle Ben!" Bryanna hugged him. "Hello, Bryanna. I am your uncle Michael. I figured Julian has never mentioned me at all. We had a falling out a long time ago." He introduced himself. He was a cop. "Honey, sit. Listen to them." Mrs. Radcliffe reached for Chanel.

Bryanna sat on the cream plush couch and studied both of the men. "So, what is the bad news?" Bryanna chokes on the words. "Why do you assume it is bad news?" Michael replies with a slight smile. "Two men coming to the door to give news. It's like you're going to tell me my husband died in a war. Given our family name, it's not far from it." Bryanna lets out a laugh back. What could possibly happen next, she thought. She starts to grow more anxious, the longer they sit there in silence. "When we were kids. We had a plan to take over the world." Michael laughs. "I was to be a police officer. Ben to be head of the world's most infamous biker gang and Julian the owner of a large company. And so, it was." Michael started the story. "Bryanna. You are the owner of The H Hotel. He gave you the majority share in the company." He then explains. "I have some shares, but it isn't enough to be the owner. And I am here now. I have a child to take care of." Bryanna informed. "I am sorry to say this, and when your sisters passed, and what happened to your parents. You have full control over the company. If you want it." Michael threw more information.

The more Michael talked, the angrier Bryanna grew. The room was tense now. Like when you torture a cow before you kill it. The meat is too tough to eat. "How dare you come here and be so insensitive about this. I never had time to grieve. I never had time to really accept it." Bryanna yelled. "You are right. We made an oath to your father to take care of his girls if anything were to happen to him. We failed him twice. We will not fail again. You want the truth, like adults? Your parents were murdered, and it wasn't an accident." Michael shattered her world. "Mrs. Radcliffe please take Chanel to the room." Bryanna's demeanor changed.

The two hurried upstairs to the playroom. "What the hell did you just say?" Bryanna asked softly. "It's true. The Roses ordered a hit on Julian and Charlotte. I guess with you in prison and your sister's dead, he moved from Savannah and guess where he is living?" Ben sits next to Bryanna. "If you say my old house, history will repeat." Rage built up in her. "The H. Where he plans on buying it. I was able to prolong the meeting enough to two more weeks. So, if you want to go home and finish this you can. You have money and you have a home." Michael handed her a box that contained the contract of ownership for Bryanna and a golden pen. "This is a phone because you need one. It has our numbers in it for any reason." Ben handed her a phone. "I will think about it and reach out when I have my decision. Thank you. Both of you." Bryanna hugged them both. "You are family. No need to thank us. Just keep a low profile. The Rose family are very dangerous. Always have been." Michael and Ben leave the house.

"You're just as bad as Grayson was." Bryanna says, knowing Mrs. Radcliffe was listening. She creeped around the corner. "How did you know I was there?" Mrs. Radcliffe laughed. "My sister was the master of eavesdropping and I always knew when she would listen. And I am kind of an expert at it too." Bryanna laughed. "So, what are you going to do?" Mrs. Radcliffe laid Bryanna's head on her shoulder and held her. "I don't know. I have Chanel to think about. I want a great life for her not knowing the family she comes from." Bryanna contested. Mrs. Radcliffe let out a sigh. "I feel like using your name in fear was actually working for your family for a long time. And when your father changed that, that is when your family started having all that drama. So, if you need to go home and get your name back, do it. Show them that a Dayton never runs. Show Chanel what it means to be a Dayton." Mrs. Radcliffe says. Bryanna knew to pull this off, she will have to play the part of a lifetime. All three sisters in one. "If you need it. I will give you mine and Ernie's share in The H." Mrs. Radcliffe offers.

Bryanna finished her shopping of business outfits and dresses and heels and more. She felt like Annabella. "You two meet me at Starbucks in town." Bryanna called Michael and summoned them to her.

She sits and waits. Eyes hiding behind her black aviators. "You know, I haven't had a Starbucks drink in two years. With good behavior." She says, sipping her drink. "It is a very good place. Especially for making decisions." Uncle Michael says. "Shut up." Ben shot a look at him. "So, why are we here sweetheart." Ben sat across from Bryanna. "What did you mean by The Rose family is dangerous?" Bryanna asks. "They have ties, close ties to the Irish mob." Ben answers. "So? We had ties to the Russians and Italians in our family history. What does that mean to me?" She asked. "They are very persistent." Michael cuts in. If I sign this contract, we need to take that family down. For good. I have seen many wars between Annabella and others and I watched how she moved around the board. If we do this, we do it my way. Not a hair out of place." Bryanna offers a deal. The two look at each other and then back at Bryanna. "You got yourself a deal baby girl." Ben shakes her hand. "And I will need something…" Bryanna shoots a quick look at Ben. "From you." She adds.

     Crystal hears a knock coming from her balcony door. Hesitantly, she looks through the curtain and sees him. "Vic what are you doing here?" Crystal pulled him inside. "You did something to me. I am like head over heels for you. I want you. Right now." Vic pulls her close and kisses her. "Then take me." She kisses him back, laying on the bed.

5. God Is A Woman

Jason always had something unique about him. He always believed he had the ability to live in the shadows, watch as someone else took over his body. When he was nine he was taken to a psychiatrist to help him with his...gift as he called it. The episodes grew less and less common but the social awkwardness grew more. He never picked up on little hints and social cues which made him an easy target for bullies and one bully turned into many.

Jason never saw a future in arts or regular life. His plan was to tolerate one more year, graduate and then off to the Marine Corps. He had a plan that would get him away from his family and everyone that bullied him, to make something of himself. He was in ROTC all through middle school and high school. He had friends. His life wasn't as sad or rough as he led people to believe. Hearing and supporting his goals, Jason's father took him to the shooting range and even started collecting different types of guns. He didn't know it would come to this...

New York mornings are busy and boisterous but no match for Danielle and her girls. Crystal sneaks Vic out of her bedroom window for the fourth time this week and gets ready for school. She slips on her leather dress over a black tee and black boots and brushes her teeth. Purple eyelids with blue under her eyes. Red lips pressed together. "Hun you're not going to eat?" Crystal's mother asked. "I'm running late mom. I'm sorry. I will make dinner tonight." Crystal started for the door. "Handsome man by the way." Her mother laughed. "He is alright." Crystal played along. "You better not get pregnant." Mrs. Lopez yelled.

"Mom, dad I know it is very much against our religion and being a Jehovah's Witness and a teenager is hard. Everyone celebrates holidays and parties and even just simply hanging out with friends. I want to spend time with friends and have a childhood. I'm always here depressed and sad." Trish expressed her feelings. "Your father and I will discuss it." Her mother brushed her off.

Amber puts the finishing touches of makeup over her face and neck. The bruises weren't as bad as others that were left before. She takes a deep breath and prepares for her journey. Three knocks at her bathroom door. "Honey." Her father asks, sounding normal. She opens the door and looks at his shoes. "You're so beautiful. Have a good day at school." He hugs her tightly as he does every other day. "I have to go. See you after school." Amber pushed him back and left before the tears fell.

Danielle sips on her Starbucks drink and sits upon her throne in the courtyard.

Unknown: Danielle, Bethany gave me your number and said that you will be giving me the money she owes me.

Me: Whoever this is, you have been played. I have never agreed or been told about this. Not sure what you have to do to her but make sure she doesn't have bruises on her face. <3

Crystal and Amber strut the halls with confidence. It has been two months since they kicked Bethany off the cheer squad and then each bullied her every week if not every day. "Morning Bethy." Crystal grabbed her backpack from Bethany's locker door and emptied it onto the floor. "Really? I thought you would have something more creative today. Dominatrix bitch." Bethany says, on her knees cleaning everything up. "Creativity takes a little time. As long as it is effective." Amber twirls her hair around her finger. "Dominate this bitch." Crystal sticks up her middle fingers pretending she's putting on makeup. "Let's go girls. Don't want to catch whatever this one might be carrying." Danielle starts off. "Hey everyone! Danielle Rose is sleeping with her teacher!" She yells in the halls. "Bethany, please speak like your thought process, slow. Everyone knows that's not true, but you were on your knees in the baseball field behind the big sign." Danielle smiles as everyone watches the throwdown. "At least I wasn't on my knees with Lucas." Bethany raises an eyebrow. "Bitch you wish I was on my knees with Lucas. It would make you feel better about your poor life choices. At least I don't give people numbers out to drug dealers that you can't pay for. Glad you found a way to pay him." Danielle laughed.

Morning Hamptonites.
    I just got a word of someone giving little Johnny Roche an oral presentation. Hope you got an A. And let's thank the photographer for the tip. You guys are so good to me. MWAH!
    TheDot.com

Image Loading....

"What is she talking about?" Danielle winks as a tear starts to build up. The girls shrugged their shoulders. "You're welcome to challenge me, but you'll lose." Danielle walked to class. "Hey Danielle." Jason had a nervous smile. "Hey there handsome." She smiled at him. "What the hell was that?" Mr. English whispers aggressively. "A cover. So, you don't lose your job." She whispered back. "Yes, I finally redid the assignment and put real work into it this time." She says loudly to deter eyes. She sits in her seat and pulls out her things. "Have you heard?" A girl hurried over to Danielle. "If I had, I probably would be in a mood. So, what is it?" Danielle says with an attitude, flipping her orange hair over her shoulder. "Your first takedown solidifies you as Queen of Oberlin." She informs Dani. "That isn't news. That is just a known fact." Danielle rolls her eyes. "Hey hot stuff, question. What is your favorite cult classic movie?" Danielle asked. "Hm, I would say Fear with Mark Wahlberg." Jason answered. "Got it." Danielle turned in her chair.

"Okay class. Today we will be taking notes on Shakespeare. Can anyone guess what story?" Mr. English asks the class. "Romeo and Juliet!" Jason belched out. "Love the confidence but no. We will be focusing on Othello. I know, I know, but Hamlet was already taken." He passes out books, grazing Danielle's hand as he does so. "Get into groups." Mr. English orders the class.

Danielle sits with Amber, Emily and Jasmine. Everyone is in groups except one girl. Spencer Loving. She was odd. Frizzy hair and she might have a slight tick. She had pasty skin and didn't have any friends. "I'm in the mood for chaos." Danielle smiles. "What do you have in mind?" Emily asks, chewing on her red nails. "A makeover. Personality and appearance. A little social project." Danielle explained. "So, what is this about exactly?" A girl asks. "Basically, about a secret marriage between Desdemona, the daughter of a guy named Brabantio, and Othello is a general in the army. Roderigo is upset because he loves Desdemona and had asked her father for her hand in marriage." Spencer explains excitedly from her desk. One look said it all from Danielle to her girls. "Spencer, come sit with us." Danielle put on her warming smile.

Clutching a book to her chest, Spencer sat with the girls in the back. "I like this *Princess Diaries* thing you have going on." Danielle comments. "I knew this was too good to be true." Spencer stood from the seat. "Oh please. That was a compliment. Sit down. It was a great movie." Danielle says in a nonchalant manner. Hesitantly, Spencer sat back down. "It is one of my favorite movies." She says, placing her hand on Spencer's. "Maybe we can hang out sometime. Give you a real *Princess Diaries* treatment." Danielle shares a comforting smile.

"Maybe we can meet at Amber's place." She added. "No! I mean, my parents aren't really ones that like having people over, remember." Amber shot out. "Okay chill OJ, it was just a suggestion. Up to you. You know where to find me. So, who wants to read first?" Danielle smiles into the book.

Carl and Crystal locked themselves in the weight room before lunch. Carl slid off his shirt and started kissing Crystal. It was different this time and she felt it. She sat on the bench and pulled up her jean overall skirt up and he pulled down his pants revealing his new boxer briefs. One leg was tight mesh material and the other side was bandage like. "Oh my god. What are those?" Crystal laughs. "What? You don't think they are sexy?" Carl joins in on the laugh while thrusting his hips. "You're crazy." She smiles as his finger enters her. "Crazy for you." He whispers. The look in his eyes said it all. Crystal kisses him to move past the awkward moment.

At the lunch table, Nate eats his fries, waiting for everyone to show up. Carl and Crystal walked into the courtyard, hoping no one caught on. "Brooo! That party was sick!" Lucas hugged Nate and sat down. "Friday's game was insane! We tore those bulldogs up!" He adds. "Thanks to Nate's playbook, we have made it into the homecoming season undefeated." Carl placed his arm around Nate. "What can I say, I have a gift." Nate jokes back. "We are having a party at my place next Friday. You in?" Carl takes one of Nate's fries. "I have a date next

Friday. Sorry." Nate informs him. "Oh yeah? Little Nate getting some? Like Lucas did recently." Carl yells out. "No no no. It's not like that at all. I really like her." Nate laughs. "Wait, you smashed my sister?" Nate asked, starting to get upset. Lucas stayed quiet and ate his fries. "Well my party is a tradition. We invite the schools and some hot bitches and just have some fun." Carl gets closer to his ear. "Maybe you can bring her. Either way, you will be there." Carl demanded, digging into Nate's shoulder. All he could do was shake his head in agreement.

Lucas happened to look over by the cafeteria to see Mr. English basically hiding from someone he was watching. He followed his line of vision to Danielle. He watched her like he owned her. "Dude why is Mr. English watching your sister like that?" Lucas got Nate's attention. "I heard he is a creep." Nate brushed it off.

Danielle sat at her table with the new project, Spencer. "Girl, ever since you gained a little confidence you've been dressing hot. I am so here for it." Danielle compliments Crystal. "Trying to be the best me I can." Crystal joked. "At the party, this girl from Upper East totally got naked fell in the pool and then tried to fight the other girls." Amber laughed, showing the video. "What? When did that happen? Before or after you went for that swim." Danielle asked, laughing. "Oh right, you both were fucking." Amber laughs. "Why does everyone keep saying that we fucked?" Danielle asks now annoyed. "You both vanished and he came out of a room zipping his pants up. What do you think?" Amber explained. Danielle started making faces into her camera. "What are you doing?" Amber laughs. "Seeing which face shows *I don't care what people think because it didn't happen* better." Danielle joins in the laugh. "So, what interests you?" Danielle asks Spencer, trying to take her mind off of it. "Books, I like watching movies. I haven't had any friends to really do much." Spencer explains, pulling at the ends of her hair. "That is a habit you will need to end." Danielle grabs her hand.

"We are your friends. We will make you one of us. We stick together." Danielle's smile soon was interrupted by a text by Nate. She looked and saw what he was talking about. George was staring at her.

Dani: *You are making it obvious.*

Loverboy: *I am just standing here. Nothing obvious about anything.*

Dani: *My brother is watching you. We will talk after school.*

"Girls, we all meet at my house today. Bring your supplies." Danielle plans an official makeover. All Spencer could do was smile. Danielle wrote down her address and handed it to Spencer.

Danielle got up and strutted over to the jocks table. "Lucas get up." Danielle demanded. He could barely look at her. "Ah! She couldn't get enough I see!" Carl yelled, nearly spitting out his juice. "Get the fuck up. Now. I'm not playing." Danielle says. Lucas now sits up, standing his ground. "Okay, you and I both know we never had sex. If we did, I wouldn't be mad about it going around, but we didn't." Danielle says. "Maybe you didn't remember it. Crossfading will do that sometimes." Lucas laughed. "Oh, so you took advantage of me? That is rape." Danielle yelled for the entire courtyard to hear. She looked at Nate who was now embarrassed. "The next time I so much as hear that rumor whispered, I will destroy every single thing you love. Understood?" Danielle stormed off.

Spencer skips through the hallway at the thought of finally being noticed. Becoming what she's always dreamed of. To be popular. To be cared for. To have real friends. She has watched as these girls took the school by force and showed no fear. Spencer wore a uniform like outfit. Knee length blue skirt, buttoned up white shirt and a gray zip hoodie. Can't forget the long white socks. "Look it is the wannabe! You think those girls will actually help you? Pathetic I think." A girl in the class says out loud. Spencer just put her head down and pulled her jacket closed as everyone laughed. Grabbing her bag, she ran out of class. Unknowingly past the girls. She didn't stop until she reached her house. The door of her room swung open and she cried. "Every time I try to be a good child of god, he tests me, and I have to fail every time. You want us to get her?" Amber asked. "No. Sometimes silence is deadlier. Let's go home and get our things. We will pick her up." Danielle started off after Spencer.

The girls stop by Trish's house to pick her up. "Come in." Trish says. "In? Are you going to like, kill us or something?" Amber asks, surprised. "Just get in here." Trish pulls the girls inside. "Hello girls. I am Trish's mother. Despite the religious beliefs we share in this household, I know you all have taken care of her. That's why I am going to give her some freedom and enroll her into Oberlin. But one wrong thing and she will be back. Understood?" Her mother makes it clear of her decision. "You have my word, she will be an angel just like she is here." Danielle lies. "Is she able to join us on giving our new friend a makeover?" Amber asks. "Yes. But not too late please." Trish's mother says as the girls jump with joy.

The girls went to get coffee when someone showed interest in Amber. "He is so cute. Please get on him or I will." Crystal says. "You can have him. I just want to focus on myself. I don't need the stress of home life and relationship drama." Amber explains. "What's going on at home?" Trish asked. "Nothing. Just normal annoying parents arguing." Amber sipped her drink. The guy walks up to Amber with a warming smile. "Can I help you with something?" She asks looking up at him. "No bu-" "Got it. Bye." Amber turns around and just focuses on the table. The girls are now shocked. "No. Oh my god Amber! He is so cute though." Crystal yells in shock as he walks away.

Hours pass, and a knock appears at the front door. She hears her mother greet someone. Or a few people. "Honey! Someone is here to see you." Her mother knocks on the bedroom door. "Are you sure you want me to let them in?" She asks next, knowing the bullying issue at Oberlin. "Yes. They are my friends." Spencer says. "You don't have friends." Spencer's little brother, Tommy says, walking into his room. Danielle, Amber, Trish and Crystal stand in the hallway holding bags. "Let's get started." Danielle pushes her into her bedroom.

They wash and straighten her frizzy hair. They get rid of the bad clothes and replace them with new ones. They teach her how to talk and walk and act. Who to talk to and who not to. They teach her the ways of makeup and then the clone of them was created.

"You look gorgeous." Danielle smiled. "She is ready." Amber says. "Oh yeah she is." Crystal adds.

Carl: Hey, wanna meet?

Crystal: I can't, busy with a project.

Carl: Come on. Finish it later, and I'll make sure you finish. I'm so horny.

Crystal: Ugh! Fine lol. Meet me in the gym, behind the stands.

The next day, the girls strut through the halls with the new and improved Spencer Loving. She was getting looks of all kinds. Anger, surprise, jealousy, happy, sexual. So, this is how it felt to be… *popular*. Her now soft and straight hair blew in the light wind current. She wore a black and white striped blouse tucked into a blue skirt. "So many people are looking at me." Spencer whispers as she sits at the table. "Good. They are seeing the power of friendship." Danielle places her hand on Spencer's. "Hey Dani. Who is the new girl?" Carl takes a seat next to her. "Spencer Loving." Danielle gloated. "Woah! You really worked magic. You are very beautiful." Carl says in complete shock. Crystal clears her throat. "Nate get over here!" Carl orders. "This is Spencer." Carl informs him. "I don't know who that is." Nate says to him. Spencer's entire demeanor changed with Nate's presence. "Both of you, shoo. We have things to discuss." Danielle pushes them away, giving Nate a look.

"Screw that girl, you're going out with us Friday, I want her there." Carl orders him. "What is this party exactly?" Nate asks. "Come and you'll see buddy." Carl pats Nate on the shoulder.

Spencer sits in class confident, head up and happy. "She thinks because they gave her a makeover she is on top of the world." One girl commented out of jealousy. "You think you're all that. They will chew you up and spit you out. Back to the way you used to be." Her friend makes a direct comment. "Can both of you stop being such jealous assholes?" Jason came to her rescue. "Thank you." She mouthed.

"Anytime. Just because they aren't worthy enough to be picked by people better than them. And prettier too." Jason laughs.

After school, Spencer walked into her house. "What is all of this? If I saw you leave this morning you wouldn't be dressing like that!" Her mother yelled. "EW! You're hot!" Her brother dropped his gummy worms. "Such a supportive family I have. What happened to be myself and make friends? I finally did that." Spencer argued her point. "Those girls are not your friends! Those girls are social misfits, living a life where all that matters are social status, clothes, boys, drinking and sexual activity. They are not your friends." Her mother tried to wipe the sinful red lipstick off of her plump lips. Spencer snatches away. "This is the new me. Get used to it." Grabbing her bag, Spencer storms off to her room. "No get back here!" Mrs. Loving yells, pushing open the door. "I swear to god if you don't let me be myself you'll lose me just like you lost dad. Do you want that?" Spencer yelled. "Wow. Very tasteful Spencer. You're even talking like them. Your father wasn't happy." Ms. Loving started to cry, banging her hand into the wall. "He killed himself because you controlled every single part of his life. You like to be in control and it hurts all of us. Be a mother for once instead of a monster. Get out!" Spencer yelled, tears streaming down her cheeks.

Hello my loves,
Haven't you heard? Miss little innocent has joined the X-Force. And it is only a matter of time we see what she really is worthy of. Will she crack under pressure or will she rise to the top? Not over Queen Danielle of course. Keep me updated.
Love, TheDot.com

It has been a week now, and Spencer starts seeing copies of her past outfits. "Is this normal?" She asks Danielle. "They love you. What can I say. Don't let it get to your head." Danielle combs her fingers through her straight red hair. "Is everything okay?" Spencer pulls Danielle aside. "People think you will be coming for my spot soon. I have to make sure that doesn't happen. Too much to handle." Danielle informs her. "What? I would never. Who even said that?" Spencer asks, confused at the mere thought. "Everyone apparently. TheDot thought it would be something to post." Danielle showed her the phone. "I am grateful to have the spot I do. I don't want to take you down." Spencer assured. "Good. I will ease off. See you at lunch." Danielle looked at the ceiling as the bell rang.

Danielle decided to sit in front of Jason today in History class. After weeks of small talk, she finally made her decision. "Hey handsome." She turns in her seat and smiles at Jason. "Hey beautiful." He says with a smile. "I was thinking you should take me out on the town tonight." Danielle suggests. "Oh yeah? And how will I contact you?" He says in a joking manner. She wrote her number and address on his paper. "The H Hotel. Seven sharp." She smiles, turning around. Carl watching from the back of the classroom.

When class was over, Carl hurried to Danielle. "So, what is it with you and the geek squad over there?" He asks. "Don't call him that. He is sweet. And can you make it less obvious that you and Crystal are hooking up." Danielle defended him. "She is fun, but I wouldn't be caught dead in public with her. My boy Lucas has like this obsessive crush over you. Give him a chance." Carl insisted. "One. Obsessive crush makes him sound like a serial killer. Two. You may have some authority over my brother, but I am not him. I bite back ten times harder. Remember that. And Three I don't date athletes. I am a cheerleader, he is a football star. I don't care for stereotypes." Danielle attempted to walk faster. "I am the star. And he could be a killer of sorts. If you know what I mean." He laughs at his pervy joke. "Get away from me pig!" She pushes him away. "I better see you at my party Friday. With Lucus." He yells in the hallway.

Danielle gets home and starts getting ready for her night out. "Dani, we need you to stay in tonight. Your mother and I are going to dinner tonight with some very important people, and Friday is the meeting to buy the H." Felton gave her the unfortunate news. "So, what do I tell my date tonight daddy?" She asks, still applying her makeup. "Well, maybe tomorrow could work. Even raincheck works sometimes. You'll figure it out." Felton kissed her on her forehead and exited the bedroom. "You are right daddy. I will." She whispers.

Seven came and Danielle met Jason in the lobby. "I should have dressed down. Sorry." He says nervously. He held a bouquet of red roses. "I feel like these were only appropriate." He lets out a slight laugh. "I hate roses." The smile quickly disappears. She starts to smile. "It's a joke. So, I can't leave the house. I was thinking we could maybe have a movie night. Order food. If you want." Danielle informs him of the new plan. "Sounds like a plan." He smiles at her. She leads him to the elevator.

Danielle and Jason strutted through the living room to her room. "Ooo, is he supposed to be here?" Nate asks, laying on the couch with his leg propped up on the back. "That is not my problem." Danielle says. "Then I am inviting Erica over." Nate starts texting her. "Do you have to be watched?" She raised an eyebrow. "Shut up!" He snapped.

"So, am I allowed to be here?" Jason asked, taking off his suit jacket. "You're fine. My father said I had to cancel my date or figure it out and guess what. I just did." Danielle smiles. "So, what do you want to watch or order?" She adds. "You pick the movie and I will pick the food." Jason picks up the menu. They share a smile as Danielle flips through Netflix.

About twenty minutes into Moana, the food arrived downstairs. "I will be right back." Danielle hurried out of her room. She walked downstairs to find Nate and Erica examining the food. One clap sent the two kids into a jump scare. "That is mine. Get away from it." She ordered. Two Xanax bars on the table. The two laughed and fell back on the couch. Eyes red as an old woman's blush sponge. "Are you two high?" She asked. "No. Yes." They blurted out, looking at each other. "Yes. No" They yelled again, switching answers in a loud laugh. "Goodbye. And Nate. Behave." Danielle walks the food up to her room.

"Why does she always make a comment about you being watched and behaving?" Erica asks. "It's nothing. I have a dark past apparently." Nate avoided the question. He looked her in the eye and kissed her. "You're mine redhead." She smiles, caressing his cheek. "All yours." He whispers back. Taking off her shirt, Erica climbs into Nate's lap. Nate kisses every inch of her body. She tastes every inch of his. Now on her knees and pushed him back and pleased him. She pulls out a condom and rolls it on. "Are you sure?" He whispers. She looks into his eyes and sees pure passion. He wasn't a monster. He was a gentle soul longing to be loved. "Yes." She answers as he enters her.

     "I just don't understand why she just had to leave her island. Why couldn't she send someone to do it? And why the chicken?" Danielle laughs. "She knew it was her destiny to save her island because everyone else was scared to." He stares at her with a certain look in his eyes. "You are different than I thought you would be." He says. "How did you think I would be?" She asks leaning back to look at him. "Stuck up, bratty, bitchy, selfish. And I will stop because this isn't first date appropriate." He laughs nervously. "I can be all of those things and more. But I try not to be." She replies. "Especially when getting revenge." She adds. "Dani?" He asks in a soft whisper. "Yes Jason?" She leans a bit closer. The room became calm. He placed his hand on her chin and kissed her. "I like you." Danielle whispers between the kisses. "I like you too." He replies. Each kiss gets more and more passionate. Jason pulls her closer and Danielle climbs on top of him. "I uh-" Jason gets anxious. "How many people have you had sex with?" Danielle asks, kissing his neck and unbuttoning his shirt. "Like, um, like, sex-sex?" Jason asks. Danielle stops and smiles at him. "Yeah, sex-sex." She laughs. "Oh. Well..." Jason cannot even look at her. "Holy shit, you're a fucking virgin, aren't you?" Danielle's jaw drops. "Is that why you want to fuck me?" Danielle asks, crawling off of him. "What? No, no. That's not it at all!" Jason starts to panic. "So, you don't want to fuck me, Jason?" Danielle struts to the middle of the room. "I do want to fuck you." He confesses. "Well, I don't fuck virgins." Danielle winks. Jason, missing the joke holds his head down. "Jason." Danielle calls, now in her lingerie. "What are you waiting for?" She asks, biting her lip.

Jason gets undressed and kisses her more. "Don't worry. I will lead this time." She says kissing down his body. He takes a deep breath, surprised at how the real thing felt. He could only imagine how it did and this was nothing like what porn made it to be. He was mesmerized by her. He was hypnotized. He was... in love. He remembered moves from the porn videos he watched every other night, morning and sometimes in the bathroom at school. He flips her onto her back and kisses her body. Her breasts. Her stomach and then he pleased her with his tongue. For an inexperienced guy, she loved how it felt. She slid the condom on him and instructed him inside. She moaned and scratched. Jason tried his best to be consistent with the rhythm but once in a while he would speed up, getting caught up in the moment or slow down to enjoy it.

When they finished, they got dressed and kissed some more. The door opens and the kissing stops. "I think I am falling in love with you." Jason says between the kisses. *Fucking virgins will do that.* Danielle thought to herself. But then she saw her opportunity. "I love you too." She says. She may have meant it a little, but she needed to remember he was only a cover. "Will you be my girlfriend?" Jason smiles. "Definitely." Danielle smiles and kisses him again. "What the hell is going on!" Felton yells. "I think I should go." Jason throws the jacket over his arm and hurries to the elevator.

He sees Nate on the couch being yelled at by Hazel. Jason and Erica waited for the elevator. "Well, this has been an interesting night." He makes small talk. "If that's the word you want to use." She replies, getting into the elevator. "Lobby also?" She asks. "Yes, please." He says, smiling at the memory of the night.

"Sit down. Both of you." Felton yells. Nate and Danielle plops onto the couch side by side. "Your mother and I leave for a few hours for a dinner that makes or breaks us and you both have people in here? We trusted you. Both of you." He continues to yell. "I don't recall you saying no one could come over. You specifically stated that I had to stay in and I will figure it out. And I did so we had a movie date." Danielle argues. "This is no time for your word play Danielle. What if something happened? And you! Kissing that girl, high. Have you not learned?" Felton directs his attention to Nate. "That was the past. Things are different now. Not that you care!" Nate gets in his face. "Stand down Nathaniel." Felton warns him in a stern tone. "Make me." Nate challenged. Hazel placed her hand on Felton's arm to calm him down, but for once it didn't work. "You think you are a big shot? Then next time something happens, deal with it yourself." Felton started to turn away. "Pussy." Nate says, provoking him.

Felton grabbed Nate by his neck and slammed him against the wall. "Don't ever try that again. Do you understand me?" Felton yelled in complete rage. "Stop! Fel. Stop!" Hazel found the strength to pull him back and protect her son. "Felton leave, now!" Hazel ordered, holding Nate in her arms. "I know what you did. We will all go down for you. We will lose everything because of you." Nate yelled almost in tears. "That is what families do for each other." Felton yells, entering the elevator.

It's not every day you see a princess with a frog, but Danielle may have a spell of her own set. Let's take a poll. How long will this last?

Image Loading....

Crystal sat on her bathroom floor and cried. Her breathing unsteady. She tried to gather herself but it wouldn't work. "Amber. Can you come over? My mom is still working and I can't breathe." Crystal struggled with the words and wiped her nose. "What's wrong, what happened?" Amber asked. "I took adderall and I can't breathe. Please help." Crystal explained.

Amber made it to Crystal's house, she entered through the back door and found Crystal alone on the bathroom floor crying and taking deep breaths. "What happened? Who gave you these?" Amber asked. "Dani gave them to me. She said they will help me lose weight safely." Crystal explains, breathing heavily. "It's okay. I got you." Amber held her close until she was able to get to sleep.

Amber sneaks into her room quietly. She reads one of her favorite books and had the TV on for background noise. She still had time, so she thought. Over the ramblings of LIVE PD, she heard things being knocked over from the table. The sound of his steel toed boots on the cold wooden floor sounded familiar. He staggered into the room next to hers. Her little brother Chase was across the hall in his room sound asleep. Her mother left minutes before he could see her like always. The doorknob turned as a tear slithered down Amber's cheek. "Hey. You're home from school already?" He asks, struggling to get the words out. "Yeah. I decided to come straight home today." She lied, breathing in deep. "You're such a pretty girl." He finally makes it to her. "Did you cook dinner?" He asks. "I didn't. But I will get started on it." Amber shot up from the seat, despite it being almost midnight, and before she could make it to the door she felt a hand grab her wrist. And then the other on her throat as her back kisses the white wall of the hallway. "You think you're better than me? You are just like your mother!" He yelled with a drunken rage. She could barely breathe. No one could help. No one could save her. So, she saved herself. She reached over and finally was able to grip the flower vase with her fingertips. Enough to be able to slam it against his head and knock him out.

A breath of relief and she ran to get her brother and a change of clothes. "Where are we going?" Chase asks. "Away for just a little while." Amber hurried getting his things together first and then hers. "Why is daddy sleeping on the floor?" Chase looked back but received no answer. They got in the town car and went to Sag Harbor, to their grandmother's house.

The two entered the mansion and waited. Their grandmother; Viola descended the grand staircase in a hurry. "Are you okay?" She asks, hugging both of them. And then she sees the neck bruises. "No. We are going to the police right now." She ordered grabbing her purse. All Amber could do was cry. Cry on the marble floor. Cry in the Range Rover. Cry in the police station.

"Where are my kids?" Amber's mother; Tiffany burst through the police station doors. "Ma'am. They are being interrogated right now, please take a seat." The officer informed. "You did this! You brought them here to embarrass me." She yells. "Your husband choked her, and from what we were told, it wasn't the first time. She had to knock him out and appear on my doorstep because she was scared. This man hit you. He hit them, and you looked away. You, their mother abandoned them." Viola explained. "You stay out of what goes on in my home." Tiffany demanded. "How can I? You are never home to do it yourself Tiff." Viola snaps back.

The police took pictures of the bruises and took her statement. She knew what would happen. He would be arrested and taken out of their home. Her family would be happy again. Before the drinking and abuse. What Amber calls normal.

The family goes back to the grandmother's mansion for the night. Silent and tense. After thinking about everything, Tiffany joined Amber on the back porch. "I want to apologize for everything. Me, not being there for you two. I guess I was just scared myself." Tiffany takes a seat. "We were scared too. You'd leave so you don't have to be near him, but because he is such a hard worker and rich you stay married. That's not love. That's why I don't believe in love." Amber refuses to make eye contact. "But it made you strong. I've watched you grow into this beautiful, strong and smart girl." Tiffany gripped Amber's soft hands. "I'm a kid. I don't need to be stronger. I need to be safe, and that is what you failed to make sure we were. Good night." Amber went to bed, leaving her mother in tears.

Amber stares at herself in the vanity. Her black and white marbled claw nails gently tracing the handprint on her neck. She isn't crying because he hurt her. She's crying because no matter what her father did, and after all that he has done, she will always love him.

After the bipolar week, Danielle sits at her vanity, curling her hair and putting on her face. It is now Friday. That means pep rally and game day. She puts on her cheerleader uniform, grabs her bag and heads downstairs.

"Eh hem." Hazel clears her throat. Danielle sees her parents at the table with Nate who is holding his head down. The table is decorated with breakfast and drinks. "Oh, so we are actually a family again or are there more secrets?" Danielle asks, folding her arms. "Let me explain. Please, sit." Felton begs. Danielle sits at the table and picks at a croissant. "I have done things to get us here that I am not proud of. I was responsible for the death of the Dayton's." Felton confessed. "Why? What was to gain from that?" Danielle asks, shocked at the news. "Look around. This is what we gained. I go to the meeting today where I will be titled the owner of the biggest hotel chain in this corner of America. A better life for our family." Felton explained. "At what cost? Your best friend's family? I always looked up to you. But, that is disappointing. I am late for school. Nate are you coming?" Danielle stormed to the elevator. "I will be right there." Nate says, words struggling through the rage that was building up. "So, I am not the reason we moved here? My actions had nothing to do with your decision. You did this." Nate commented. "No son. I paid that family off to keep their mouths shut for what you did! You assured my decision. Now get to class and no more of these outbursts." Felton escorted Nate to the elevator. "You guys are Rose's. With this blood comes dark history and darker decisions to stay where you are in life. I love you both more than life itself." Felton kisses their heads.

"My love. Today will change our lives forever. When I get that hotel, we will never have to worry ever again." Felton kisses Hazel. "We will be legends. Taking over the world." Hazel kissed him passionately and then he was off.

The board meets in the boardroom. The white collars are organizing their files and sipping their coffee. Men and women sit in silence, waiting for the president of the board to come in. He is followed by Felton Rose and his son Donovan. "Alright, everyone. Hopefully this is the last meeting for this topic. You brought it to my attention that leaving The H under no ownership will be a bad look. What makes you believe you can handle this chain?" Marshall asked, writing something on his notepad. "The last family to own this hotel was, well let's just say it. They were messy people. I mean kidnapping, scandal, adultery, secrets, murders, embezzlement and fraud. It is time for a family with no ties to Russian mobs or blood on their hands. And to be honest, they aren't even here to fight for it." Felton's cocky tone lit up the room.

Suddenly the door opened, and Bryanna Dayton strutted into the room like her sister would have. Black office skirt suit. Following her, the horsemen. "I am hurt that I was not invited to my family's board meeting. No worries, I am here now to claim what is mine." Bryanna says. "You can't just walk in here with your gang of ingrates and ask for handouts." Donovan yelled. Felton grabbed his arm. "No, it's okay. Do you want to tell him Felton? Or shall I?" Bryanna smiled. "This company is actually my great grandfather's. That was founded and ran and passed down by the Dayton lineage. Since I am the last living Dayton. It was left to me with the largest percentage in it. So, this company is mine and you all work for me now." Bryanna slid the contract to Marshall.

At that moment, Felton's world fell apart. The room fell silent. Felton held back the impulse to strangle her for taking what was almost his. "This is actually... all facts." Marshall looks over the contracts. "Nice to have you Ms. Dayton. Welcome home." Marshall says. "My deepest apologies Mr. Rose." He adds. Everyone leaves the room except for Bryanna, Ben and Felton and his son. "This is far from over." Felton threatened. "You may have caught my parents off guard, but I was raised in war. Just know. A Dayton is not one to cross. Have a great day." Bryanna flashes a smile and orders security to escort them out. "Oh, and you need to be out of the penthouse as of Tuesday morning… I'll be generous, Tuesday night." Bryanna ordered. "Good luck on all of your future endeavors and your job search. You're fired." Bryanna smiles. "Now I see why Carissa did what she did." Donovan says exiting the room.

Bryanna visits the Dayton Mausoleum, leaving roses and Annabella's favorite peonies there. She lit a candle for them and cried. "God. Why did this happen?" She cries out. "I'm taking on the biggest role yet. Please guide me through this. I am avenging our family and reinstating our name. I need you guys. Chanel needs you guys." She begs. Even though she was never big into religion, she says a prayer and heads back to her home to rest.

"I have something for you." Ben handed her a black box with a beautiful red bow. She started to open it. "You didn't have to." She says, pulling out a black leather jacket. The Horsemen symbol on the back. "With or without the jacket, you are one of us." The rest of them entered the room, leaving the judging eyes of the employees. Bryanna handed the jacket to Ben. "Family is family." She smiled. Ben put the jacket on her. Bryanna flipped her hair out and strutted out of the boardroom and to Julian's old office. Her office. It was just like he left it. Nothing touched. "I miss you so much. Guide me please." She whispers. Then there he was. Devon Morris, smiling at her.

Jason and his father took a trip to their favorite spot to blow off steam. It was an outdoor gun range they built on his grandfather's ranch. Jason took his AK47 and hit every target with ease. "So who is this lucky girl that's got you in love." His father asked. "Her name is Danielle. She is so beautiful and sweet and sometimes assertive but overall a good person. She is proof that god exists." Jason pulled out his phone and showed off her picture. "A girl like that will get you in all sorts of trouble. Just be careful bud." He warned. "I was worried at first, but I trust her. I'd kill for her." Jason smiled, going back to shooting the targets while his father watched in worry.

"Ms. Kuvly, I apologize for the last-minute meeting. I am in a difficult situation and I need a place to actually settle. A penthouse isn't really my... Taste." Felton explained to the real estate agent. She stood tall in her black red bottoms. Her hair in a tight bun and her blue dress twirled with every step she took. "Nonsense. It is always good to help someone find their dream home. You can call me Debby." She caressed his arm. "So, this is what I like to call authentically barn style façade. Beautiful modern interior. Wooden flooring is absolutely beautiful. Vaulted ceilings and walls of glass that really bring the outside in. If you're an outdoors person like myself." She explained, escorting Felton through the home. "The living room is anchored by my favorite, a grand fireplace with a custom cedar mantle. The open entertaining area flows seamlessly into what I like to call the 'barn room' with soaring ceilings and beautiful beams. This space is centered around a large eat-in kitchen with a beautiful marble backsplash and two large islands as well as a wet bar with an additional sink, ice maker and wine fridge. High-end appliances." She explains. They go through the rest of the house. Six bedrooms and eight bathrooms, the pool and backyard and garage. Now back in the living room they go over the details. "Hey love, sorry I am late." Hazel struts into the home. "You must be Hazel. I was just telling Felton here about the details of the home. You are welcome to look around if you like." Debby smiles. "I trust my husband's judgement." Hazel smiled and took a seat next to Felton, giving him a hello kiss. Debby sighed and cleared her throat. "This home is shy of six million. Totaling over 7,000 square feet of living space on three levels." She wraps up. "We will take it." Hazel says as she pulls out her checkbook.

Bryanna met with a man that she had only seen once and from a distance. "Your father once made a deal with us to do business in this hotel." He says. "Maxim Chernov. You want to run drugs through the hotel. That will not happen." Bryanna said, motioning her men to leave the room. "Russian mobs. Drugs. Violence. My dad loved it. My sister did also. But I am not them." Bryanna sat on the table next to Maxim. "You are the new leader of the Russian mafia. Congrats." Bryanna slid a key in an envelope to him. "I knew you would come eventually. I bought a warehouse for you guys. Keep a low profile. And stay out of my building." Bryanna ordered. "I will be in touch." Bryanna struts out of the office. "Yes, I am calling to see how the investigation is going." Bryanna says, getting into the elevator. "I know Felton Rose killed my parents. I know he will try to kill me. Keep me updated please." Bryanna hung up.

6. Thorns of a Rose

When Amber was younger, her family were very close. They went out on trips and had dinner every night. Her father, Marcus was Junior CEO at a bank and her mother Tiffany was a high profile real estate agent. They lived comfortably and stayed in contact with other family members regularly. Things were... normal for Amber. She had friends and good grades and even helped in the community like gardening and at the senior citizens home.

Over time, Amber experiences the normal life like when she was twelve she met a guy named Alex Derringer. He was tall for his age and sweet to her. He joked and looked out for her, until middle school when he asked her out and then dumped her for Bethany at an eighth grade party.

The kids sat in a circle waiting on the beer bottle to stop on the lucky two people. Alex and Bethany sat side by side giggling and flirting. In an impulsive rage to make Alex jealous, Amber shut her eyes. "Lucas and Amber! Closet for seven minutes!" The girl yells.

The kids shoved the two in the closet and closed the door. "I guess we just sit here until it's over." Lucan says. "My ex is out there having the time of his life with a new girl. I just want to get back at him." Amber says. "Who is your boyfriend?" Lucan asked. "Alex freaking Derringer." Amber. "Then let's give him a show." Lucas took advantage of the moment.

Within those six minutes, Amber lost her virginity to none other than Lucas. She didn't like him and he didn't like her in any way. They helped each other get out of the V-card club. The moans and bangs against the door let everyone know what was going on inside. In that moment, Amber stopped caring. She stopped caring about her anger towards Alex, her love for him, the innocent girl she held on to. They exited the closet and with a smile looking back at all the kids' shocked expressions, Bethany staring at Alex who was crying in anger and jealousy, Lucas' smile of satisfaction. Amber strutted out of the party and went home.

That was the night that Amber's uncle was found in his car, dead. Alcohol was the cause that was told to Marcus and alcohol is what consumed him also. It consumed his happiness, his family and Amber's normal world.

It only took less than ten minutes to take The H away from Felton. It took an hour for Hazel to buy a new home in The Hamptons. "What do we tell the kids?" Hazel asks. "That we found something more stable. We aren't going anywhere. Call the movers." Felton kissed Hazel on the forehead, admiring the new home. "It feels like home." She whispers.

During the last period, Danielle snuck off to the bathroom to fix her makeup. "I must be the luckiest man on earth to see you here." Lucas appeared behind her. Backing her into a wall. "When are you going to give me a chance? I can't stop thinking about you." His face moves closer to hers. "Get away from me Weinstein. You are aggressively pursuing me and it's creepy." Danielle rushes back to class. Lucas gave a thumbs up and Carl pranced around the corner. "We got this bitch." Carl laughs.

Danielle entered the bathroom to someone crying. "Are you okay in there?" She asked. "I'm fine." A girl replies. "Open up." Danielle knocked. A girl opened the stall door revealing her black eye and bruises on her body. "Don't tell me Bethany abused you." Danielle snickered, soon realizing that's exactly what happened. "What happened? From the beginning." Danielle ordered. "Well, this has been going on for a while. She told my dad I was gay and he kicked me out of the house. And her mother doesn't know any of this. She gets so angry, she threw me into a wall and it just got worse and then she dumped me. I lost everything for her and I was just a secret. She is able to walk about and start over. How can I?" She started crying again. "You can't.

All you can do is learn and move on. I will handle it. What is your name?" Danielle stood up in anger. "Jess." She replied.

Danielle met her friends in the locker room after school and crushed up the Molly she pulled from her pocket. They lined them up and snorted them. The bells rang, and it was time for the game. They all were dressed in their cheer outfits and faces made up with their FENTY, Urban Decays and ANASTASIA products. "What do you use to make you so shiny and sparkly?" Amber asks. "Fenty body lava. Here." Danielle stood behind her and helped apply some. "Rihanna?" Amber asks. "The queen herself..." Danielle trailed off seeing some of the bruise marks on her neck. She quickly helped apply it before anyone could see. Who could have done this to her? Danielle asked herself. "If you ever need anything, do not hesitate to come to me." Danielle whispered. Amber couldn't look at her. All she could do was look down at her fingers.

"These are the girls." Bethany showed her mother in the locker room. "All so beautiful. You must be Danielle." Bethany's mother asked. "Smart. I am." Danielle rejected the handshake. "Well, the hazing stops now. Do you understand me?" She took a step forward but that didn't intimidate Danielle. "You know, after getting a text from that drug dealer about you not paying him and that I have to, I was willing to let it go and then hearing that your ex girlfriend was beaten and thrown into a wall, that took the cake." Danielle snapped. "You're gay?" Bethany's mother asked in shock. "You're off the squad if that isn't obvious. Now shoo." Danielle waved them out of the lockerroom.

Eight came around and the game was coming to an end. Danielle was on the field with her girls in their cheerleader uniforms.

Hidden in the stadium was George English. Not caring for the sport or the students, except one. Lucas on the field watching Danielle ever so often. And Jason working the concession stand. "You. I'd like water. Cold. Thank you." Danielle says "Dani, she doesn't work here" Amber laughs. "Then she's not busy." Danielle replies. "Hey cutie." Danielle bounces up to the stand. "Hey there beautiful. What can I get you from my wall of wonders?" He jokes making his voice deeper. "You are such a nerd. Can I have fries?" She hands him a few bucks. "On the house. I got it babe." Jason says, handing her the cup of fries. "Are you sure?" She asks hesitantly. "Yes. Here. Kiss me. Maybe we can celebrate our two months tomorrow?" He leans through the window and kisses her. Snap! A picture is taken. When Danielle opens her eyes, she sees George walking into the school. "I would like that. I gotta run. I will see you later." She takes off after him. "Hey nerd. How does it feel to be played?" Carl asks. "What do you want, Terril?" Jason started to get angry. "Just the truth. You think a girl like her is really interested in you? The last thing I want to do is hurt you." Carl says. "Says the guy who pantsed me and dunked my head in the toilet last year." Jason contested. Carl held up the phone and showed the picture. "The nerds never get the girl." Carl laughed and walked away.

Lucas met Danielle in the hall again. "Remember when I called you a creep? This is now stalking. Lucas, go away." Danielle pushed by him. "Who the fuck do you think you are?" Lucas yelled. "Excuse me? No one important to me is what you are." Danielle folded her arms. "You flirt with me and then you ignore me and then you tease me and then you leave. Then when you need something you want to flirt again?" Lucas crept up to her. "So, if we're not gonna fuck then what are we doing?" Lucas asked. "Okay, you must be delusional." Danielle let out a slight laugh. "So, this is a joke to you? Danielle, you think I'm here because I'm interested in you? In what you have to say or your feelings? You're not fucking interesting, okay? You are just a hot cheerleader that I wanted to smash. Fuck, you are so stupid." Lucas laughs. "And you are just another airhead jock that won't make it anywhere in life. You came on to me, remember? And ever since then, you show up, you pour your desperation on me, and then you whine about how your day went like I cared. Like, every time you start talking, I think to myself, who the fuck does this guy think he is? You are the one that's so fucking boring." Danielle stormed off.

Nate sits on the bench during intermission, catching his breath. "What school is this again?" Nate asks. "NorthShore Prep. Upstate New York. You know..." Carl plopped next to him. "You killed their player." He whispered with a smirk. And at that moment, the announcer blared through the mic. "Can we all have a moment of silence for a fallen player. We lost our beloved Elijah Ethans earlier this school year. He will be missed, loved and never forgotten." The players stood in a straight line with their heads held down. A few of them limped over to the Knights team. "No matter what happens tonight. If we win or lose. We know one of you is responsible for Eli's death. Remember, they are always watching." The player taps under his eye and walks away. Nate looks at Carl. "Whatever you are going to say, don't. We finish the game. We have my party. We sleep it off." Carl orders.

Danielle enters George's classroom. "Knock knock." She says flirtatiously. "So, you're done kissing other boys and ready to be with a man?" He asks, annoyed. "You know we have to keep us a secret. So, if people see me dating him, you are in the clear. You keep your job and I keep you." Danielle sits on his desk. He wraps her legs around him and kisses her deeply. "Why are you so addicting?" He starts kissing on her neck. "I could say the same about you." She moans. His hands start to explore her body, inside and out. "We have to stop. Not here. We will finish this." She fixes herself and leaves back to the game.

Walking back to the stands, Danielle passes her father. "Daddy. What are you doing here?" She asks, surprised. "To support you both. Your mother is in the stands too." Felton informed her. "I had a chance to talk to your boyfriend. He has a good head on his shoulders. Whatever game you are playing with him. Try not to hurt him." He whispers. "Trust me daddy. It is honest, unlike you." Danielle can see right through his veil. "What are you talking about?" He asks. "You came here because something happened. I have picked up on your behavior over the years. I am not stupid. What happened?" She asks. "We were kicked out of The H. Your mother and I have it under control. We bought a house where we will be moving into tomorrow morning." Felton explained. "What happened to buying the H?" She asks, trying to piece everything together. "Bryanna Dayton was released early without probation and took the company back. Leaving me with nothing." Felton answers. "Then we take her head on. She stole the company from us. We aren't leaving without a fight." Danielle kisses his cheek and joins her girls.

Nate runs with the ball. Ducking and dodging the other team trying to tackle. He threw it to Carl who was open. As instructed. Carl scores the winning point. The stand roars with excitement. Two teammates lift Carl up onto their shoulders. "Yeah baby! We did it!" He yells. "Good game!" Lucas slaps Nathaniel on his ass. "You too man! That pass was sick!" Nathaniel says, throwing his arm around Lucas. "Hey, congrats on the game." Spencer ran up to Nathaniel. "Thank you. Are you going to the party at Carl's later?" Nate asks. "I wasn't planning to. Why are you going?" She asks in a flirty way that obviously went over his head. "I may make a cameo. See you later though!" Nathaniel runs off to the locker room.

"Ladies let's go get some food I am starving." Danielle flips her curly orange hair over her shoulder. "Will I be able to see you tomorrow?" Jason hugs her from behind. "We are actually moving tomorrow. If you want to help." She explains, kissing him. "I'm there. Text me." He runs back to close the stand. "It is so odd." Crystal says. "What is?" Danielle looks at her. "You are the head cheerleader. I picture you to be with Carl or another athlete." Crystal answers. "Cheerleaders dating athletes are overplayed. It's like we are expected to. Expect the unexpected. I always say." Danielle smiles. "And Carl seems to be spoken for." Danielle winks at her.

Crystal runs up to Carl and his boys in excitement. "Congratulations on the win Carl." She smiles. The team looks at him and starts snickering. "Thanks." He turns towards them and laughs. "Seems like all the girls want you. Playa!" One teammate yells out. "I don't do fat girls. Not my thing." Carl answers. Soon looking back at the hurt Crystal standing in the same place.

Carl: *I'm sorry. Please come to my party tonight. I'll make it up to you.*

Crystal:...

Erica hugged Nate after the game, congratulating him. "Your hair is purple." He says with a slight laugh. "I wanted to try something new and crazy. Also, I have a surprise for you." Erica smiles, taking a step back. "As of Monday, I will officially be a student at Oberlin Prep." She jumps up and down from excitement. "What? That is awesome!" He holds her tightly and kisses her. "So, this is the lucky lady." Nate's smile vanished quickly. "Erica, this is my... friend Carl. Carl this is my girlfriend Erica." Nate smirked. "So, will I see you at my party tonight?" He asks, stepping closer to her. "Yeah. We will be there." She combed her bangs back with her fingers. "Good. See you soon." Carl smiled, patting his shoulder. "Why did you tell him that?" Nate asks, storming off. "What was the big deal? It's a party. It will be fun. And it'll be a way to make friends." Erica tried to explain. "You don't understand. He isn't a good guy." Nate aggressively whispered. "Then why are you friends with him? What does that make you?" She asks. Nate didn't have an answer. "Exactly. You know what, I am going to go home. See you tomorrow." Erica stormed to the town car.

"Fuck!" Nate kicked a trash can. "Nate." Felton appeared behind him. "Sorry dad." Nate held his hand down. "Get control of your anger. We do not need anything happening right now. We are at war. Come on. We are going to what is left of home." Felton threw his arm around Nate and escorted him to the parking lot. "What do you mean?" Nate asks his dad. "The Dayton's are the owners of The H again. Bryanna Dayton was angry that we were after her family's business. She kicked us out. We move into our new home tomorrow. I just told your sister a few minutes ago." Felton explained. "What is our next move? Kill her too?" Nate stood up straight. "We keep our hands clean." Felton orders. "Dad, I have to tell you something." Nate knew what he had to do. "Nathaniel Rose?" A police officer asked. "Who is asking?" Felton stood in front of Nate. "We need you down to the station for questioning. For the murder of Elijah Ethans." The second officer handcuffed Nate and took him over to the rest of the team in handcuffs. "I will meet you at the station." Felton hopped into the car with Danielle and raced off.

Nate sat in the interrogation room alone and anxious. Tapping on the metal table. "Hello. My name is detective Bennings. My partner, Johnson. Do you know why you are here?" Bennings asks Carl. "I am not sure, honestly." He answered confidently. "You were accused for the murder of Elijah Ethans." Detective Bennings informed him. "I don't know who that is." Nate says. "I was informed you were attending the same party the night of his death." Johnson stated. "I was at Carl's party. We were at his house. Sleeping over. His parents were there. The other teammates were there." Nate avoided the question. "So, you did not go anywhere at all before your party?" Bennings ask for assurance. "We were at my house. Food and drinks and snacks were bought before the all nighter. We weren't in the right state of mind to do anything." Carl lets out a slight laugh. "I think that is all for now." Bennings releases Nate into the lobby. "Dude! Finally. We are gonna be late to my party!" Carl pulled Nate towards the exit. "Not tonight boys. Nathaniel needs to go home with me." Felton stopped him. "Yes sir." Carl backed down for the first time. "Aw, where is the glass? I would have loved to see you behind it. Maybe even place my hand on it and say something like stay strong or we will get you out soon, like in one of those Lifetime movies." Danielle laughs. "This is a police station not a prison, and I bet you would." Nate snaps back. "Knock it off, both of you." Felton ordered.

Felton got into the car with Nate and Danielle and started home. "Did you do it?" Felton asked through a sigh. Nate looked at his hands. Felton got his answer. "Don't worry about it. We will take care of it." He says in a stern tone.

Carl's party was in full effect. People in the pool and jacuzzi. People dancing in the house and smoking and doing other drugs. Bottles of Everclear, Skol and LTD sat around the house. Music blared through the house. People playing beer pong in the backyard. "Dev, Max, Jonny, Will, My room." Carl ordered.

"This is the party we all have been waiting for. Better late than never. Rules are, find a girl, bring her back, cameras are set up. And take names. Scoring book starts tonight!" Carl yells. The guys leave the room on the hunt for girls. Drunk girls, drugged girls, easy girls, it didn't matter. Until one girl caught Carl's eye. "Well, well, well. You know you can't visit my home without giving the host a kiss. Kidding. Where is Nate the great?" Carl jokes. "He isn't here?" Erica asked, looking around. "We had a fight and I figured he would be here." Erica explained, pinching the bridge of her nose. "Oh, that is why he is upset. He is upstairs in my room. How about I get you a drink and I take you to him." Carl bargained. "Then why did you ask where he was?" Erica waited as he returned to her with a red cup. "What is it?" She asks, smelling the poorly mixed drink. "Rum and coke." He explained looking around. She saw the blueish particles inside. "Uh, those guys are fighting." Erica pointed behind him, soon pouring her drink into his. She then put the cup to her lips as if she actually gulped it down. "Where is your bathroom?" Erica asks. "Follow me." She smirked as Carl took a swallow of his drink.

The two walked up to the room and saw the other girls and guys having sex. The girls didn't look like they were awake. "What is this?" Erica tried to back up. "Stop being a tease. This is what you wanted. I saw it in your eyes." Carl backed her into the door. She threw his drink in his face and kneed him. Running out, taking the book of names. "Get back here you bitch!" Carl yelled, chasing her into the party. "Are you okay?" Spencer asked. Everyone watched. "Let's get you dried off. Where is your bathroom?" Spencer led him upstairs and through the open bathroom door, closing it behind them. Jealousy enraged Crystal, causing her to storm out of the party. Amber, following to see what was wrong.

Spencer sat Carl on the toilet and found the soft white towel. She pats his face gently. "You smell so good." He whispers, pressing his face into her chest. "Thanks. Are you sure you're okay?" She asked looking into his eyes. Carl starts to feel her arms and then her face as he kisses her. She tries to pull away. "What are you doing?" Spencer asks. Carl pushed her to the door and started kissing her harder. She couldn't fight back. His hand pulled up her dress and she felt a finger inside. She knew what was going to happen. He bent her body over the sink and violated her. Deflowered her in the most violent way. She tried to get out of his grip, but she was too weak. She begged him to stop, but he didn't listen. All she could do was wait until he was done. Maybe he will get bored. Or maybe... hopefully someone will come in and save her. Her friends will save her. Nate will save her. Her mom? His mom? Tears fell down her cheeks like bombs.

Moments pass and he finishes and stumbles out of the bathroom. She runs out crying. No one cares. To them, she asked for it. To them, she wanted to hook up with the coolest guy in high school. She ran home. The August breeze in her hair. The blood on her yellow sun dress, running down her leg. Some stained her white converse. "Mom!" She screamed through the tears. Her mother jumped at the disheveled girl with messed up makeup and bloody dress. "What happened?" She examined her up and down. She knew. A mother always knows. "I was raped." She tried to piece together the words. Rage building up as they poured out of her red, smudged mouth.

7. The Bird and The Worm

Growing up, Carl was pressured by his father into striving for a career in football. He underwent very intense practice sessions before school, at football practice and after school and sometimes on weekends. Though he hated his father for his methods, Carl believed his determination would one day translate into his very own success.

During his high school football career, Carl held the state record for most receiving yards in his sophomore year and broke the school's records for most receptions, most yards during a game. He was cocky from the very beginning. He always got what he wanted through manipulative tactics with the females and assertive control with the males. His team accepted and respected his alpha role no matter what he did. In reality they didn't want to lose the frat boy lifestyle he blessed them with, the vacations and the treatment they received around town. Girls flocked around him, even knowing he was a complete womanizer. Carl never dated and always paid close attention. He knew a threat when he saw one. And he knew just how to get rid of them.

His mother worked in an office but attended every game and was always there for him. She was the sports mom that everyone adored. To her, Carl could do no wrong, but Carl knew exactly what he was capable of. And he knew he was untouchable.

"My daughter would like to file a report. She was just raped." Spencer's mother says to the NYPD. They took them into a room and asked them questions.

"What happened." Detective Johnson asks. "I went to a high school party. And I was raped." Spencer explains. "How are you so sure you raped?" He asks. Another Detective joins in. "This is Detective Jones. She handles these kinds of cases more than I do. I feel as if you'll feel more comfortable speaking with a woman. You can take over." He leaves the room. "Hello. I am Detective Jones, but you can call me Lana. Tell me what happened." She explains. "I went to the party looking for someone." Spencer started. "After being lured there." Her mother cut in. "I saw Carl Terril. He didn't look good. Some girl he was chasing threw a drink at him. He took me to the bathroom and locked the door. I didn't think anything of it. I dried off his face and shirt." Spencer says. "To be clear, you removed his shirt?" The detective asks. "No. No clothes were removed." Spencer answered the question. "All of this is new to me. The parties and dressing like this and having... friends. It was like I was just a pro..." And then it clicked. It was all a game. A set up. They all did this. "...project." She whispered. "They all set me up." She says, tears starting again. "Who? Who set you up?" Lana asks, pushing the recorder closer. "**Carl Terril. Danielle Rose. Trish. Crystal. Amber, Erica** and **Nathaniel Rose.**" She listed the names. "Do you have last names for the others?" Lana wrote them. "I can get them. Nathaniel lured me there." She added. If it was anything she learned from Danielle, it was how to tell a really good lie to start a scandal. "We need to take samples. We will need to get you to the hospital." Lana instructed.

Saturday morning, The Rose family made their big move into their new home. "This is gorgeous." Danielle takes off her cat eye sunglasses. Her red curly hair blew in the wind. "Just like you." Jason smiled, kissing her. "Box, kitchen." Felton stepped in. "We came here to move in. Not to tease boys." Felton commented. "Good thing I learned multitasking from the best. Juggling lies and secrets." Danielle smiled that smile that says *Oh yeah, I went there*. "Cut it out. Now. We don't have time to be fighting. People are after us. We need to stand together." Felton comments. The movers continued the rest of the move and then the police entered the driveway. "The truth might be out sooner than you thought daddy." Danielle gloated. The black cars stop abruptly. "Danielle Rose. Nathaniel Rose. We need you both down at the station." The officers put the twins into the car and headed to the station. "What? What's going on?" Danielle asked but no answer.

Bryanna sits in her new office and learns the ways of the company from Michael. "Bry, Mike. There is someone wanting to be a part of the horsemen." Ben informs. "Well we will meet this person tonight at dinner. My parents always said, a home is not a home until you have a Dayton dinner party." Bryanna crosses her legs. "Words of mother." Ben snickers. "Out of the fifty thousand dinner parties' mother has held, you have attended two." Michael contested. "That is not true. I have been to three." Ben playfully argues back. "You crashed one. So, I will settle with two and a half." Michael smiles. "Well, you both get ready for tonight. This will be a formal event." Bryanna assured. "I assume you will be bringing Devon." Ben says. "I've seen him leaving your room." He added. "No, I will be going alone." Bryanna laughs.

The company employees were finally coexisting with the gang members. No fights or killing. Everyone was professional. "You are a natural born leader. You have brought together a biker gang and professional business men together in peace." Michael watched everyone in the office. "I am doing something my father didn't. And that is why everyone is at peace." Bryanna explains. "Here you go. And here you go." The assistant handed them the coffee. "Did you hear anything recently from our enemies?" Bryanna asks, sipping on her coffee. "The twins were arrested. The parents are planning something big. If you are going to make a move, you need to play a card now to set them back." The assistant informs. "Thank you." Bryanna gives her a smile of appreciation.

"Why are we here?" Danielle asks, annoyed. "Well, I am detective Bennings. I heard you are friends with Spencer Love. Am I correct?" Bennings asked. "Yes. Why? What did she do?" Danielle sits up straight. "Something happened at Carl's party. This is an investigation." Bennings informs. "I want my lawyer." Danielle ordered. "Just tell me what happened. Where were you?" Bennings changed to a softer tone. "I was here. They called me in for questioning and I went home with my dad." Nate blabbers. "Did you tell Spencer to go to the party?" Bennings ask. "No. I told her I might show up there. And I was going to go with my girlfriend. I did not tell her to go to the party. What happened?" He states. "She was raped. And she named you and a few others. This is an investigation now." Bennings informed. "I didn't do anything to her." Nate slammed on the table. "Calm down Mr. Rose. Now, or we will place you in cuffs." Bennings threatened. "We need to know who your girlfriend is, so we can have her in for questioning." Bennings added. "Why do you need her?" Nate asks, calming down. "We need everyone that might have witnessed her there. The more you cooperate with us, the faster we can get you guys set free." Bennings wrote on her notepad. "Erica Worthington." Nate sighed. Donovan sat next to Nate silently writing everything down.

"Ms. Worthington. You were at the party, correct?" Bennings asked the purple haired girl. "Answer honestly." Her mother commanded. "I was there." Erica says. "And did you see Spencer there?" Bennings writes on her notepad. "I am not sure who that is." Erica shook her head in confusion. "Well she knows you." Bennings slid a picture of her on the table. "She was at the game. She said she was going. I do not know her though." Erica explained. "You didn't know her enough to place a drugged drink in her hand?" Bennings looked at Erica. "What? Erica, tell the truth now!" Her mother ordered. "Was it that Rose boy? I told her to stay away from that family. They are worse than the Dayton's." Her mother added. "Nate wasn't at the party. He told me not to go because Carl was a creep. I went anyway. Carl pretty much was a nice guy and got me a drink until…" Erica trailed off. "What happened Ms. Worthington?" Bennings asks. "You guys are going to hate me. Carl made me a drink and dropped something in it. He didn't know I saw. I pointed at a fight and poured my cup into his. He took me up to his room and said Nate was up there waiting for me. Nate wasn't at his party though." Erica explained. "So, you roofied Carl in his attempt to drug you. What was in the room?" Bennings started to write something on the pad. The room fell silent. She placed a black book on the table. "There were other football players having sex with girls. I am not sure if there is a video. He says it's tradition. I know because my sister was involved in this tradition. I thought Annabella Dayton was bullying my sister from like jealousy, until I saw their names in the book. Annabella's name was crossed out instead of checked marked. They were drugged. He slammed me against the door. I kicked him and ran out of the room. He ran after me and pulled at my arm. I threw my drink in his face and bumped into a girl, but I was not stopping." Erica finished. "Spencer was raped. She says it was Carl." Bennings informed. "I wouldn't be surprised. I should have listened to Nate. He didn't want me to go. I thought he just didn't want me to make friends, but I see he was protecting me." Erica dropped her head into her hands. "Go home and rest. We will be in contact just in case." Bennings escorted them out.

Passing the lobby, she sees Nathaniel. She runs up and hugs him. "I should have listened to you. I am so sorry!" She cries in his arms. Everyone watches them. Spencer's mother enters the station. "What happened at that party?" Nate asks her. "Please don't get mad." Erica says. "This is serious Erica. What happened?" Nate asked sternly. "Carl tried to drug me and rape me. I ran out after he tricked me to go to his room. He said you were waiting for me." A tear ran down her cheek. She saw the rage build up in him. "Son." Felton placed a hand on Nate's shoulder. "Did he touch you?" He whispers. "No. I left before he could." She struggled through the tears. "Glad to see someone taking this seriously. If it wasn't for you, my daughter would be home." Ms. Loving accused Nathaniel. "Ma'am I only had one conversation with her. I don't even know her." He contested. "You too. You and your whorish ways corrupted my daughter. You slut!" She pointed at Danielle. "I understand you are extremely upset. But, you will not talk to my children like that or you will have a bigger problem on your hands. Do you understand me?" Hazel threatened. "Is that a threat? Mrs. Rose." Ms Loving asks. "Yes. A mother will go to any length to protect her children. Now back off. Let's go, children." Hazel orders.

Back at the finished home, The Rose family has a meeting in the living room. Donovan and Elizabeth included. "Liz, hun can you give us a moment?" Felton asks. "She is a part of the family now. I trust her." Donovan says. "Things have gotten out of hand. That Dayton bitch has taken the one thing I needed to make our family expand. I will not stop until I get it back." Felton banged on the table. "What do we do?" Elizabeth asks. "Take that family down. Once and for all. And we can't do that when you two are in the spotlight." Felton answered. "I did nothing wrong but make a girl have friends. I did a good deed. Nate is the one in the spotlight." Danielle corrected him. "I wasn't even at the party!" He says. "But, you possibly killed someone. Someone said they saw you. If it is true or not, you are the face of an investigation." Felton explained. "Especially since we are here because of your actions in the first place." Danielle shaded. "That is not helping." Donovan whispered.

"It isn't supposed to help. Remember what you are capable of doing. Just be lucky a higher power kept you from that party." Danielle says. "Bryanna will play dirty, but she isn't capable of going low to exploit someone. She got what she wanted and thinks she is untouchable." Felton thinks out loud. "We need to find out her secrets and exploit them. Her sister already confessed, but she has more. Talk to people in that prison. We will get this bitch." Felton says.

Danielle sits at her vanity fixing her hair. A knock appeared at the door. Nate. "Yes?" She asks. "Why do you hate me so much?" Nate asked. "I don't hate you. When I look at you I see a disgusting trash of a boy that shares a bloodline. But I don't hate you. Every time I look at you I question what I could have done to stop you that night. Every time I miss home and I want to talk to someone I remember I can't. You ruined my life. But, we are family. So, when I am mean to you, when I say the things I do, it is because you not only ruined my life. You ruined theirs too." Danielle explained. "It was the biggest mistake of my life. I didn't mean for any of this to happen." Nate started crying. "Save it and get out of my room." Danielle turned back to the mirror and watched him walk out of the room before her tear fell.

The phone rings. Bryanna rushes to pick it up. "Sammy it is almost midnight. What is it? What happened?" Bryanna asks, sneaking out of bed, trying not to wake Devon. "Take a seat because this will blow you away!" She says. "What news do you have for me?" Bryanna listened and smiled a smile she has seen Annabella make too many times. The ammunition she needed.

      "My name is Jada Masse and I saw something happen to Elijah the night of his party." She says to the New York police. "What do you know?" The officer asked. "Do you want the full story or just the Reader's Digest version?" Jada shot a look at them.

Part 2.

THE ELEVENTH HOUR

ROME WASN'T BUILT IN A DAY, BUT A DAY WAS ALL IT TOOK TO BURN DOWN.

8. How Do You Solve A Problem Like The Rose's

"Recent news has been released regarding the rape of a teenage female. The party at the Terril's residents turned out to be more than she expected when the alleged football star raped her in the bathroom. It has been said to be more than a house party, but a traditional hazing by drugging girls and sleeping with them against their will. The investigation is still ongoing." The news reporter shouted. "I am off!"

Nate says, walking towards the door, uniform in hand instead of on. "Why aren't you wearing your football uniform?" Danielle asks, fixing her curly half ponytail. "I quit. I don't need to be around what they are about. It is not who I am anymore." He says. "I will go with you." Danielle grabs her bag and they are off. "You don't have to Dani." He holds his head down. "I am still going." She followed.

The two siblings walk into the locker room and into the coaches office. "Coach. I can't be on the team anymore. It is too much going on. I need to focus on school." Nate put the uniform on his desk. "Abandoning your brotherhood will end badly. Especially at this time." Coach says. "Roses are strong. Let's go Natey." Danielle pulls him out. Before walking out, Carl slams Nate into the locker while Eddy and Lucas holds Danielle back. "Get off of me you disgusting pervs." She yells. "You leave this team. I tell everyone you killed that boy at the party." Carl threatens. "Tell them. Because if you retract your statement from the police we all go down. So please tell everyone." Nate laughs. Carl punched him in the stomach and threw him down and they proceeded to jump him. Lucas and Eddy jumped Nate, while the screams of Danielle went ignored.

The guys finally stopped and walked out of the locker room. Danielle helped him up and out of the locker room. "Let's get you home." She struggles through the tears. "No. They are not going to run me out of Oberlin. This is our school now. Let me be a part of your crew." Nate struggles through the pain. "Yes. You're in." Danielle hugs him. "Let's get you cleaned up." She holds him up and walks to the girl's bathroom.

She pats his bloody and bruised face with a damp tissue. "I meant what I said." I never meant to do it. I wouldn't hurt anyone." A tear fell from his eyes. "I know. Don't ever speak about it in public." Danielle says, throwing away the tissues. A girl barges into the bathroom, Amber. "Dani. Nate. You need to see this. Now." She panics. "What is it?" Nate asks following. Passing the "RAPIST" spray painted in silver on Carl's locker. There it was. Painted on Nathaniel's also.

Hello Oberlin. It's been a while since something this big was exploited. Well, Georgia's Rose, Nathaniel was keeping a huge secret from us. He indeed is a rapist and for the first time the family of the victim is speaking out. If it's hard to comprehend, here is some help. *Once there was a pretty princess named Brielle, she was liked by many under the wing of Danielle. Invited to a party and drank pretty hardy and raped by a drunken prince named Nathaniel.* Sound familiar Rose? Remember when I said what goes around comes around? What are thorns, when you are stepped on by boots?
- Love TheDot.com

Everyone stood and stared at them. Two speechless siblings in the middle of the hall. "Leave them alone!" Jason and Mr. English escorted them to the dean's office. "Your parents were contacted. We will discuss it more when they get here." Mr. English had his hand around Danielle. "Thank you. I can take it from here." Jason pulls her closer. "How are you babe?" Jason asks. "I am fine just... in shock." She pulls away. He started feeling like she wanted nothing to do with him. "Should I go?" Jason asks. "Yes. This is a family matter. I will text you." Danielle kisses him and closes the door behind him. "Well now the world knows." Danielle says. Her phone kept blowing up with notifications. "Do you want to check that?" Nate asks. "Why? I already know what it will say." She replies. "Are you alright?" Mr. English caresses her arms. "Yeah we will be fine. Thank you. Go teach your class." She shuts the door behind him. "Don't do it." Nate says.

The room fell quiet for a moment. "Do what?" Danielle asked, knowing what he meant. "The student and teacher scandal isn't something you want to be attached to. The way he looks at you and how he hides in the shadows around school and lunch to watch you is weird." Nate explained. "He watches me at lunch?" Danielle asks in shock. "Are you okay? What happened?" Felton busted through the door. Danielle shows him the text. "This was sent out to all of the students in surrounding schools." Danielle explains. "What is going to happen?" Nate asks, crying. "We will handle it. Don't worry." Felton held him. "Mr. Rose. We have a lot of parents calling in about your son. I think it is best that he takes up virtual school until we make our final decision." Headmaster Rogers entered the room and informed the family. Felton started to get angry. "If my brother gets kicked out, then Lucas, Eddy and Carl needs to also, for jumping him and assaulting me this morning in the locker room." Danielle argues. "Get them in my office." Rogers orders his assistant. "We will take care of the other boys. Danielle, head to class and Mr. Felton, we will be in touch." Rodgers exited the room. "Dad I can come home if you need me." Danielle insisted. "No. Stay here and finish the day. We will figure something out. Thank you honey." Felton hugs and kisses her forehead.

Danielle makes her way to class, everyone hushed as she passes. "She probably helped him." One student whispers. "Do you think she knew?" Another whispers. She sees her girls and she sped up. "This morning has been hectic." Danielle sighs, finally making it to her friends. "Listen, Dani. You can't be a part of this group anymore. Your brother is a rapist." Amber says. "From now on, I will be taking over the group." Crystal smiles, fixing her clothes since she lost weight. "Expect the unexpected. Isn't that what you always say?" Crystal laughed as they strut away. Another Rose taken down.

Well, well, well. Seems like the Rose's are being plucked out of the garden. Hope they can survive without water.
-Love TheDot.com

"I know that bitch is behind it. I just do." Hazel says, walking out of the Gianvito Rossi store. That is when she saw her. "Please. Mrs. Loft. Don't do it. He is just a boy." Hazel begged. "And that gives him a right to get away with it? My daughter is my world. Justice needs to be served. This is the check for the forty million. Your hush money was never used and never will be. Your son deserves to rot in hell. Now get out of here before my daughter sees you." Sabine Loft handed her the check and walked into the store.

Hazel raced home to her husband. She fought through the reporters and paparazzi. "Where is Nate?" She asks in a panic. "They suspended him from school. He is in his room." Felton explained. "I saw her. In the city. They will be doing an interview." Hazel informed him. "Who?" Felton asks. "Sabine." Hazel covers her face. "It is just a scare tactic. They will not do it after accepting that money." Felton snapped. Hazel handed him the check signed by him. "We will have to do something." Felton whispers. "We didn't make as many friends as we should have because you wanted to keep it business. The Daytons had parties and events to build allies. This family is alone and surrounded." Hazel started crying. "Even I lost all my friends at school because of this." Danielle struts into the house, mortified. "You guys turn on the television to Darcey Mann." Donovan storms into the house.

Felton does as instructed. There she was, Brielle Vandermen. She had her black and brown hair curled to the side. She wore a navy pants suit. That familiar butterfly necklace. "It is great to have you here today. How do you feel?" Darcey Mann asked her. "I feel better. I feel stronger." She says in a sweet tone. "That girl is all but innocent." Felton yelled at the television. "That is really good to hear. Talking about this is not easy. So, I will just let you tell the story before I ask any questions." Darcey leaned closer on the white couch. Nate watched from the hall.

"Well, I was best friends with Danielle Rose. She was the popular girl of the school. She had her clique and I was a part of it, they made me feel... wanted. We were friends for years, like all of elementary school to high school. One night we were going to a house

party. I dressed in a black dress and heels. Did my hair and makeup and left. While we were there, I danced and socialized. I saw Nathaniel Rose there, I said hi because we were friends, our families were extremely close. He handed me a mixed drink. I accepted. People ask me why I accepted it. Like I said, we were friends for years, I went on vacations and sleepovers and I have trusted this family that has never ever done anything to hurt me. They treated me like I was their family. Until that night. So, the party went on and there were some older kids doing drugs. Like cocaine and weed. I just had a mixed drink and danced. I saw Nathaniel starting to pass out, so I literally took him to the bathroom and stuck a toothbrush down his throat and forced him to throw up. I didn't know what he did exactly. I just knew he was drinking before we arrived. Every time he came around drunk I would help him and make sure he doesn't get in trouble. Same with Danielle. I was like the mother of the group. So, he turns around and stumbles into me. He gives me this...this look. It was strange. It wasn't a romantic look. He pushes me against the door and tries to kiss me. He has never made a pass at me before. We never shared any feelings other than brother-sister type of feelings. Only little jokes and compliments. I told him to stop and tried to push him off, but he was a football player that worked out every day. My little self cannot push that much muscle off of me easily. His hand slid up my dress and I heard his zipper open. I begged him to please stop multiple times, but he ignored me. I tried to fight, but..." Brielle trailed off. Her closed eyes started to drop tears like hail. The audience were crying and sniffling.

"He placed his hand on my throat and told me to stop now or else. He proceeded to rape me. I told my parents the following morning. My father insisted we met with his parents. My father didn't want to get the police involved since I was drinking too. I found out that his parents paid my father to keep quiet and then they moved.

Forty million reasons to hate that family in one check. When I saw Spencer's story I had to look deeper into it. When I saw the connection, we couldn't keep quiet. As much as I hated it I respected my father. I didn't think I had a voice. Especially since my father and his father worked hand in hand. I understand why he made the decision, but I can't keep my silence, especially with the Me Too movement. Forty million or more is not worth the mental state I had to endure for months. My mother left my father and took me with her." Brielle explains what happened.

"I reached out to a judge on my own. Judge Morris. He said word for word. Nathaniel came from a great family, excellent school, with astonishing grades and on the sports team. Pressing any kind of charges would destroy the boy's life. And then he kicked me out of his office. I was alone and couldn't do anything about it." Brielle added.

Darcey takes a deep breath. "Wow. That was powerful. I cannot believe your father accepted money over your wellbeing. I am so sorry. So, this family decided to pay your family and start fresh in a new city. He was able to start at a new school and he even has a girlfriend and is living a good life, but have you moved on? Have you been able to live life normally again?" Darcey starts getting upset. "I have not." Brielle answers. "Exactly. This issue should not go unnoticed. Especially when the same thing happened with his friend and teammate at his new school. What is the coincidence? The Rose family went to extreme lengths to hide a rape. Ladies and gentlemen. When is enough, enough? She is a teenager trying to enjoy her young life and was punished for helping what she thought was a friend." Darcey yells now. Danielle leaves the house. "Remember You have a voice no matter what!" Darcey says before the cameras turn off. "Thank you so much for sharing your story with the world. It was very brave." Darcey hugs Brielle. "Thank you for giving me the opportunity to." Brielle smiles. She makes her way to her dressing room.

She changed into a pair of jeans and a pink sweater. "Honey. I can never express how sorry I am. I was supposed to protect you, instead I protected them." Ms. Loft started to cry. "We needed the money. I understand. It is okay." Brielle joined her in the cry. "I will go get the car ready." Her mother walked out, patting her eyes with a tissue.

The door opened and closed. Brielle heard heels clicking slowly towards her. Reapplying makeup in the tiny mirror, she felt a familiar presence. She turned to see the ghost from her past. Her black hood covered half of the famous orange hair. Her perfectly made up face. Those red lips. She wore a black button up tucked into a plaid red skirt. Brielle's favorite outfit. Her Michael Kors purse dropped onto the floor. The girls, under a moment of weakness ran to hug each other, which Brielle knew was now out of character. "I am so sorry. No one told me until it was too late. Why didn't you tell me?" Danielle asked. Brielle's mother listened at the door. In a rage. "He is your brother. I was a friend. Blood is thicker than water." Brielle says in a sigh. "No! Wrong is wrong Brielle! I have yelled at him and expressed how much he not only ruined my life but yours. What he did is inexcusable and disgusting. And I did tell him that. I remind him every chance I get. Brielle you are and always will be my best friend." Danielle sways over to the mirror and fixes her makeup. "I miss you every single day. I just wanted to say never think you have no choice. Because you always will. Blood isn't always thicker than water. I know it might mean little to nothing and I am not the one that should say it, but I am so sorry." Danielle gave her one last hug and grabbed her bag and walked out. "Danielle." Brielle's mother stopped her. "I am sorry. I just... wanted to see her." Danielle looked at her shoes. "Thank you for being a good friend. Don't treat Nate like he is dead. You are all he has. No matter what he did. Be the girl I knew in Georgia." She hugs Danielle. "It is hard. I will try, but she is dead. I buried her myself. But I had to dig her up. She isn't the same. She'll never be the same. Please take care of each other. Goodbye." She gave up fighting back tears and ran down the hall.

Bryanna sits at her desk, looking over new plots and potential spots to open new hotels. "You just think you are smarter than everyone." Felton appeared at the doorway. "What are you talking about?" She smiles, closing her laptop. "Oh no. By all means. Stay on your shitty computer!" Felton rushed over and opened it, holding Bryanna by her hair. The yelling alerted the office. Ben entered, now aiming a gun at Felton. Bryanna holds a hand up. Security handles him to the ground and starts to escort him out. "You ruined everything!" He yells. People start recording. "I ruined everything? You murdered my parents. You took away what I loved the most. You and your rapist son can share a cell. And I'm the one who shared that detail with the press." Bryanna yelled in front of the world.

Hello My loves. More to share. The reigning Queen B has taken some lessons from her sister. A takedown is a takedown no matter how old you are. But, the truth is out. Felton Rose killed the OG Dayton's. Nathaniel is a rapist and Danielle was spotted at Brielle's interview… why? It took years to take down a Dayton.

A rose can always be plucked out of a garden. Don't worry B, we always root for the Dayton's.

-TheDot.con

Donovan picked up Felton from the Hampton PD and took him back home. "Dad, what the hell were you thinking? That was a stupid move. Now the police are investigating. FBI will be involved." Donovan yelled. "I was just angry. She is picking apart our family, one by one. She has something on us, and we need to find it and take it." Felton yelled in the car. Pulling up in the driveway. "No dad. You are picking this family apart. The police will be looking into every single thing you have done. They will be tracking you. They will be watching you. And it doesn't help that Nate and Dani are now in the spotlight. They have a fucking crazy wall with all of our pictures and news clippings and notes and shit. God dammit! You need to end this war with that Dayton. Now." Donovan beat the steering wheel.

They walked into the house and smelled something burning. Felton runs out back to see Danielle at the fire pit. "What the hell are you doing?" Felton turned her around. "That bitch ruined our family. I don't want anything from that family in my closet!" Danielle snatched away and added another dress to the fire. She squirted more gas on the flames. "We need to take her down. For good." Felton whispered behind her. "And then what? We move again?" She asks, focusing on the flames. "Anywhere you wish princess." Felton replies. "One step at a time daddy. I am going to cause hell at my school. I learned from one of the best." Danielle says in a dark tone.

9. "Warnings"

Unlike thrill rides, funhouses are participatory attractions, where you enter and move around under your own power. Incorporating aspects of a playful obstacle course, they seek to distort conventional perceptions and startle you with unstable and unpredictable physical circumstances within an atmosphere of wacky whimsicality.

Prom is coming, and the students of Oberlin were starting to get excited. A night in Paris was the theme. Now that Carl and Nate were out of school. Danielle almost had the school back on her side. She started stretching in the gym as Amber and Crystal entered. "Hello crime sister." Crystal jokes. Amber laughs. "Girls you both are late." Danielle points out. "Well with all of the mess you are going through-" Crystal started. "You might not like me or want to listen to me. But, I am the captain of this squad you have no choice. Today we will be doing a full body workout. Get outside and run up and down the bleachers." Danielle ordered. "I can't do that. Doctors' orders." Crystal says. "The doctor can suck my dick like you were doing to Carl for months. Get to it now!" Danielle snapped. "Bitch I'll have you cancelled on Twitter."

Crystal threatened, pulling out her phone. "Go for it. I'll let them know about your new coke problem." Danielle winked.

The girls worked out for two hours non stop. Danielle gathered them all in the grass. Drenched in sweat and out of breath. She handed the girls water but held two in her hand. Then slowly opened both bottles and poured them into the grass. "You two are no longer on the team. You can leave the uniforms in the locker room and be on your way." Danielle says. "Dani, I need this team for college. Please." Amber. "Geez. With my rapist brother. I don't have control over my life. Just messy. This is my game. The old Queens may have taken their sidekicks back time and time again. But, I needed you two and you committed treason. This is war. You're welcome to challenge me, but you'll lose." Danielle strutted to the locker room.

In a fueling rage, Crystal walked to the field where she saw Jason. "Your girlfriend is keeping a few secrets from you. Maybe you should ask her for the truth. And if you think she loves you or even likes you, then I am sorry. It was a dare we all made." Crystal storms off. Jason turned to Danielle in anger and pain. "What did that bitch tell you?" Danielle asks. Jason just turned and walked away. "Jason! What the hell?" Danielle pulled his arm. "You lied to me, you played me, this was a joke to you, but I actually thought I had a chance." Jason yelled, snatching away from her. "Jason. Lied about what?" Danielle asked. Jason just kept walking. "Doesn't matter. This was all a game anyways." He stormed off.

After the long week of gaining a little respect back, Danielle can finally breathe in the hallways. She stood alone. She ate alone. She was alone. Her brother was gone. Her friends were gone. She had no one.

Jason dumped her. She ate lunch in the study room, alone. "May I come in?" Mr. English asked, tapping on the door. "It's school you don't have to ask." She answered looking down at her fries. "Are you okay?" He sits down next to her. His hand gently pushed her hair back. "I am alone. No one wants to be my friend or have anything to do with me." She starts to tear up. "I am sure that isn't true." George whispers, placing his hand on her back.

Jason barges in, seeing enough. "Get away from my girlfriend you creep!" He yelled, pulling him away. "Knock it off!" Danielle pushed Jason off. "Now I am your girlfriend? You have dumped and avoided me all week and he actually cared enough to check on me. As far as I know I am single, you made that very clear. You are a freak. Just a game we played to see if you'd actually fall in love with me, remember? You are pathetic. I never loved you and I never will. How could I ever really be with a freak like you? No one likes you here. Just a toy to play with in my free time." Danielle knocked her tray on him and stormed out of school as everyone laughed at him.

After school, Crystal was grabbed and pulled into an empty class room by Carl. "Did you give me something?" He asks angrily. "What the hell are you talking about? You're not even supposed to be here!" She asks. "I went to the doctors and had to get a shot. You nasty bitch! I trusted you. Don't ever talk to me again you pig." Carl pushed her against the wall. "Are you being serious?" Crystal started crying. "You raped Spencer and the cops are after all of us. Because of you. You're the nasty one. You are scum. Now stay away from me." Crystal yelled, running into the hallway. She had to find the nearest bathroom. She felt sick. So sick she could throw up. No. This was actually throw up coming. Crystal rushes into the girls bathroom and shoves her head in the toilet.

      She hurried to the nearest clinic and waited in the lobby. At that moment Crystal realized it didn't matter how great her yellow crop top looked or how the glitter laid on her pink eyelids, she was alone. She filled out her paperwork and took a number. What could it be? Was it life threatening? Will she die? Her mind started racing. Suddenly her chest started tightening and it was hard to breathe. No matter how many deep breaths she took she couldn't shake the thought. She couldn't tell her friends, she couldn't tell her parents. She had no one. She watched as other men and women and teens cried as they entered and exited the back room. The nurse calls her number and escorts her to the back room. "I am going to ask some questions and I want you to be as honest as you can with me. This is strictly confidential." She says, getting out her tools. Crystal shakes her head and takes a deep breath. "Are you currently sexually active?" She asks first. "Yes. Mostly hookups. But I have been careful. I've only slept with one guy that hasn't used a condom. The other's I have because I don't know them." Crystal answers. "How many guys have you slept with in the past year?" She asks, scribbling the words down. "Honestly more than twenty. But not all of them were sex sex. Sometimes it's oral or just fingering." She explains. "Why do you think you have something?" She asks next. "I was confronted by the guy I hook up with regularly that he had something and believed I gave it to him. But I don't have any symptoms or feel any different. I think it was an excuse to stop talking to me." Crystal wiped a tear away. The nurse takes blood and walks in another room. "Sometimes the carrier won't get symptoms for years. So they won't even know they have anything until it's too late." The nurse explained.

Returning, the nurse brings a small cup. "We need you to pee in this just to make sure nothing else is there." She explains. Crystal does as asked and hands it to the nurse through the door. "So how long does it take?" Crystal tucked her black hair behind her ear. "A few days. Can I ask something?" She asks. "You just did." Crystal laughs, trying to make light of the situation. "You are a beautiful young woman. Why hookups?" She asks. "I'm fat. I know I am. But I am confident. I've spent my entire life afraid that people were gonna make fun of me because I was fat. Afraid of hearing it. Also went through half my life with comments and people laughing at me. Honestly, who gives a shit? There's nothing more powerful than a fat girl who doesn't give a fuck. I hooked up with him because I believe no matter how popular, or- or sexy or, or great you think a guy is, they're actually all just fucking pathetic. I didn't think I would grow feelings for him. He called me names and refused to be seen with me because I am fat." Crystal realizes it. "No one deserves that. And you can't do that to yourself. You have a bright future ahead of you. Save it for someone who is worth it." She placed the gloves hand on Crystal's. "Thank you." Crystal whispers as the beeping goes off.

Tonight was the Hampton carnival, and Crystal returned her retro 80's look for it. Her fishnet stockings raced up her legs under the short jean shorts, stopping right above her exposed belly button. She slid over a yellow cut off sweater. "Socks on or off?" She asked Vic. "Off." He answers, admiring her. She slid on her leather black boots and straightened her vintage glasses. "Let's go cutie." She smiled. Vic was a perfect distraction. For a grungy biker type he treated her better than any man ever has. She liked that type, always has. Danny from

Grease, Ponyboy from The Outsiders, even Jughead from Riverdale. How they treated women, how they loved their girls. She dreamt about it for a very long time. Little did he know, she would fuck everything up in moments. He liked her a lot. If she didn't know any better, she thought he would kill for her. "Have fun! And Crystal, be safe." Her mother yells giving her the eye.

Amber arrived at the ticket booth with Trish and Chase and waited for the others. "So who is this Vic guy?" Trish asked. "She said she met him at this bar we went to a while back. She seems happy." Amber checks her phone. "That's good. She needs to be happy. She deserves it." Trish comments. "We all do." Amber looks up and sees them. "Hey bitches!" Crystal dances up to them and hugs them tight. "This is Vic, Vic this is Amber and Trish, my best friends." Crystal introduces them as they enter the carnival. "Hey little man, want cotton candy?" Vic asked Chase. "Yeah!" Chase jumped with excitement. Vic and Chase started over to the food area. "What anything babe?" He asked. "I'm okay right now." Crystal smiled.

"Okay, I love this glow you have and he is so cute and makes you happy. You are happy, right?" Amber smiled. "Blink twice if no." Trish jokes. "Yes. He is so sweet and fun and he likes me for me. That's all I could ask for honestly." Crystal answers.

Nate and Danielle entered and people stared at him. Some were shocked that he had the audacity to show his face. Others gave him dirty and nasty looks. "I told you showing up would be stupid." Nate started towards the exit. "They need to know you aren't that person. Show them you aren't." Danielle stopped him. "Can I see your phone?" Nate asked, holding out his hand. She unlocked it and handed it over.

"Fine. I'll go get food. If you need me shoot me a text." Nate walked off. Danielle spotted Dallas by the bar.

"Hey you." Danielle struts over to the bar. "Hey. Thirsty? What can I get you?" Dallas smiles. "Remember that drink you made me at the last party we met at. That one." She smiles. "Ah. I got you." Dallas pulled out a red cup and poured sprite inside and placed a cardboard holder around it, slipping the molly inside. "That will be twenty." He informed her. "Thank you cutie." Danielle took the cup and walked behind the Balloon Pop game and crushed the pill in the bag before snorting it from under her freshly done claw nail.

Carl and Lucas strut around like nothing happened at all. It wasn't fair how some people protected him over Nate, but that is the hypocrisy of high school. The longer you know someone, the easier it is to blame someone else. "Who is this lucky fella?" Carl walked up to Crystal smoking from a handmade one hitter. "Not someone who mistreats women." Crystal snapped back quickly as Vic pulled her closer. "Please do not engage with him." Amber comments. "Why not? I mean she wasn't acting like this when we were hooking up." Carl dropped the bombshell. "I'm sorry, what?" Amber spat out. Carl knew what he was doing. He told them because he knew she wanted that. "It was only a distraction. I mean, you kept running back. Before I committed myself to Vic of course." Crystal returned fire like no one was around. "Well, we know I can satisfy you a lot better than this dirty greaser." Carl stood his ground. "Excuse me?" Vic shot out of his seat. Crystal held his hand. "Carl, get away from us. Don't you have someone else to bother?" Crystal rolled her eyes. "Fine." Carl laughs, walking off.

Crystal stormed off to the nearest bathroom stall and took some deep breaths, trying to pull herself out of a panic attack. A few knocks on the stall, Amber attempted to calm her down. Danielle watched from the sink mirror, fixing her hair. "Crys, are you okay? Crys open the door." Amber called out. "Can you help me Dani?" Amber asked. "You all casted me out. That isn't my place anymore." Danielle left the bathroom.

Danielle entered the fun house alone. The house was dark with the occasional strobe light. Every room is different from the one before. She reached a room filled with mirrors. Suddenly she was backed into the mirror and kissed. She knew by the kiss it was George. He was dressed in jeans and a plain T under the black hoodie. His hand slipped under her skirt and a finger inside. Something clicked. She didn't want this. She wanted to leave but his grip was strong. "I...I can't tonight not here. Not now." She let the fake tears drop so she could hurry out. George looked into the mirror and punched it, screaming in anger. Danielle has teased him all year. He shook his head in understanding of what he had to do and exited the house. One person saw it all. Trish ran out of the house, pushing through other people entering. "Wrong way!" Someone yelled. She looked around but all of her friends were gone. "I know you saw what happened inside. Please don't tell anyone. I fell into temptation. It was a mistake. I will do anything please. Just don't tell anyone." George appeared behind her. "I don't know what you are talking about. I ran out here because I feel like I am about to throw up." Trish was always a bad liar. She ran off to find Amber.

"Look, it's our little buddy." Carl plopped down next to Nate. Nate kept his head down. "You know, it sucks that you quit the team. I would have loved to give you another black eye." Carl laughs. Lucas made eye contact with Nate. He knew he didn't want to do that to him, but he felt he had to. Nate stared at Lucus with disappointment and hurt. Nate got up and walked away without a word. Defeated he felt.

Pulling out his phone, Nate did something he should have done a long time ago.

Nate: *Brielle, I know I am the last person you ever want to hear from. But I am so, so, so sorry for what I did. Or what I didn't do. I was supposed to protect you and I ended up hurting you. It was NEVER my intention to do that. I was confused and figuring things out. I was intoxicated and dealing with my own demons. It is not an excuse. I just want you to know I am truly sorry. I'm sorry I took advantage of you. I am sorry I didn't keep you safe. I am sorry it took this long to apologize for my actions. It kills me every day knowing I not only hurt a close friend and family but the girl I... Loved. You don't need to forgive me. But just know I am sorry for all of it.*

B:
B: *Thank you.*

Vic entered the bathroom and knocked on the stall. "Babe. Open up." He says. She opens the door, revealing the smeared blue and purple makeup. "I'm sorry. Just hate him so much." She cries. "Look at me. Don't worry about him. Focus on us. I am here, right here. I'm not going anywhere." Vic pulls her face closer and kisses her. "I love you." he whispered. Her face dropped. She never heard those words directed to her from someone other than family. "I love you too." She says quickly. "Let's go home." Vic smiled.

Carl: *Meet me behind the faris wheel in five.*

Crystal did what she thought was the right thing and showed Vic. Vic grabbed the phone and walked out of the bathroom. Maneuvering through the crowds of people, he makes his way to the meeting spot.

"Finally, I thought you..." Carl stopped at the sight of Vic. "Usually I would beat the fuck out of guys like you, but I know Crystal wouldn't want that. She is happy with me, I don't play mind games with her, I care about her and show her off like the Queen she is. Leave my girl alone." Vic knew what kind of guy Carl was, he had to be careful about what he said. "Yeah? Or else what? You gonna call yo gang on me homeboy?" Carl baited. Vic laughed and headed back to Crystal.

Amber exited the bathroom to a missing Chase. "Chase? Chase!" Amber called out. "There you guys are. I just saw-" Trish was interrupted by Amber's yelling for her brother. "He is missing?" Trish asked. "No I'm just yelling for sport. Please help me find him!" Amber snapped. "Calm down. He is around her somewhere. We will split up and search for him." Crystal snapped back. "Chase!" The girls yelled in different directions. Their screams get lost behind the loud music. The lights started to mix together and the crowd grew.

Danielle made her way through the crowd and bumped into Trish. "I know you probably hate me, but Amber's brother is missing and she is freaking out." Trish panicked. "First, have you heard of the most?" Danielle asked. "No why?" Trish blinked with confusion. "Because that's what you're doing right now. Last time I saw Chase was over there by the parking lot with some man." Danielle stated. Trish ran off to the parking lot. "Amber. Dani said Chase was with some man in the parking lot! Meet us there." Trish informed.

Trish found Chase being put in the car with Amber's dad. Danielle stood behind the car and Trish in front. "Move!" Amber's dad yelled to Danielle as she crossed her arms. Nate saw the commotion and saw the man try to back over Danielle. "Hey! You're trying to hit my sister?" Nate yelled. "Nate, he is trying to kidnap the kid." Danielle informed. "Dad? What are you doing?" Amber asked. The kids surrounded the car, forcing him to get out. "You think you could come here and kidnap that child?" Crystal asked. "He is my son. It's not kidnapping." Her dad argued as Amber got Chase out of the car. "This doesn't help your case. You beat us every day! You hurt mom! The next time you come near us I will call the police." Amber yelled, confessing everything in front of everyone.

Her father sped off into the night as Amber stood in the dusty parking lot. "I know. It's okay. You're okay." Danielle hugged her tight, not acknowledging Crystal. "I will let them take you guys home." Danielle walked off with Nate.

"Why didn't you tell us you were being abused at home?" Crystal pulled Amber in for a tight hug. "It's not really something you like to bring up. It's fine. My mom and grandmother are taking charge of the living situation." Amber explains. "Let's get you home. Wherever home is." Crystal says.

Exactly three days and four hours had passed and the nurse finally called. "So good news and bad news maybe." She says. "Good news first, to soften the blow." Crystal prepared for the worst. "You are very lucky. You are STD free. Just need to be more careful." The nurse started. "And the bad news?" Crystal sat up straighter and took a deep breath. "You're pregnant." Those words shattered her world. She couldn't hear anything after that. Everything was just blurred. What is she going to do? She can't keep this child. She can't. She can barely make it through life herself. She hurried into the bathroom and threw up. "Thank you. I uh, I have to go. Thank you." Crystal says, falling against the wall and crying.

After exactly seventy-three texts and twenty calls and multiple Instagram and Facebook messages later, Crystal showed up at Carl's house, Banging on the door. "What the hell do you want toxic waste." He asked, snatching the door open. "I went to get tested. I was honest with her. You weren't the only guy I was sleeping with. But was the only guy I wasn't safe with." She confessed. "Good to know you are a slut." He started inside. "I am clean. So whoever you got it from, wasn't me. But I am carrying your child." She shots out. "What did you just say?" He crept closer to her, shocked. "You heard me. I am carrying your child. I am untouchable now. You want to hurt me? I will show you hurt." Crystal laughed walking back to the car when she received a text.

Vic: *Let me take you out tonight.*
Crystal: *I'd like that. Eight?*
Vic: *I'll be there.*

With a rage, Carl slams the front door and rushes to his room. He sits on the edge of his bed and cries. Not from sadness. From the sheer fact that his career and life can be changed forever. She now had power over him and everyone will know. He looks at his computer and gets an idea. She wants war? Well he will show her what a war lord could really do.

10. TIME STANDS STILL...

It is here. A night in Paris. Danielle sat at her vanity applying her makeup. Her perfectly painted face, her scarlet red lips rubbed together. Her red Hamda Al Fahim dress hung on her closet door. Hazel studied Danielle from the doorway. "Years of struggling to see over the sink to watch me put on my make up and now you do make up better than me." She crept over to her. "I learned from the best." Danielle smiles.

"Beautiful as always. Shouldn't your date be here?" Nate asks, leaning on the doorway. "I will leave you two at it." Hazel exits the room.

"Jason and I broke up. I am going solo. Now get out I need to get dressed." She pushes him out of the room. She took a deep breath and slid the dress on.

Her heels clicked on the cold floor as her parents waited with smiles. "Honey you are so beautiful. absolutely breathtaking." Hazel smiled and hugged her tightly. "You get in there and you show that school what the Rose family does best." Felton kisses her forehead. "Thank you. I won't be back too late." Danielle laughs, entering the elevator.

Danielle entered the limo with her cheer team and they were on their way. The music blared in the limo as the girls and their dates drank, screamed and joked. Danielle couldn't help but feel like something was off. She took out her mirror and reapplied her red lipstick. Took a few deep breaths. "Are you okay?" One girl asks. "Yes. Everything is fine. Just thinking about who the king and queen will be." Danielle put on a fake smile. Danielle pulled the little weed she had left and her golden blunt wrap and packed it. "That dress is beautiful." Another comments. "Thank you. You all look so gorgeous tonight." Danielle smiles, but she can see the lies that glowed in their eyes. She lit the joint and took a puff. Opening the sunroof, she blew out of the limo. "Anyone want any?" She offers.

The ride to Oberlin finally ended and the girls and their dates rushed inside, leaving Danielle all by herself on the steps. How did it come to this? Everything she wanted, gone. Everything she was trying to avoid happened. What would Annabella Dayton do? She asked herself. She entered the venue and saw everyone sitting and talking to their peers. The table she was placed at was filled, but one chair was filled by someone that must have been lost. Spencer was in her seat. "You must be lost, or illiterate. I mean we all know you are a bad liar." Danielle approached Spencer, anger built quickly. "You have some nerve showing your face here." Crystal says, brushing off her coral colored dress. Crystal then held on to her date; Vic. "Why wouldn't I show up? It is my prom as well." Danielle asks with her sneaky smile. She had a card. A card that will make or break her after this. "Because your brother is a rapist." Spencer yelled. The room fell silent. Danielle turned around. "Yes. My brother is a rapist. He raped my best friend at a party while drunk. And he is paying for that, I had no part of it whatsoever. So, bullying me, harassing me, will stop." Danielle shot back. "And if I don't?" Crystal stood face to face. "I'm not above violence." Danielle whispered, taking a step closer. "I'm sorry, was that a threat?" Crystal yelled, alerting everyone. "Yes. It was indeed. If you think for a second that I am afraid of you, you have been traumatized tremendously. This confidence you have. Remember who gave that to you. And I can surely take it away." Danielle laughed.

"Everyone, this girl lied to the police and said my brother was involved in what happened to her when he wasn't even near her. She was not raped. Maybe she was, but not at that party and not by my brother. Then again it doesn't matter because you were just upset. Upset at me and everyone at this table. You told the police we all lured you there when we did not. We made you interesting. You were invited to the party. But we didn't lure you in any way. You should be ashamed of yourself." Danielle yelled at Spencer. Tears rushing down her face. "You told the police we lured you?" Amber asked. "What I did to Jason was horrible, but I would never lie to get someone arrested on false charges. Now get your ass out of my seat. And you get your ass out of my school." Danielle ordered. "Clearly one of us has underestimated the other." Bethany says.

Spencer shot up and ran into the hallway, crying hard. Danielle sat down and fixed her hair. "Why are we all still looking around? Get back to prom, talk. The show is finished." She snaps her fingers. "I am sorry. For everything." Trish whispered. "We have two months left until summer. And then I will find a new school and make new friends. I thought you girls would be my best friends who wouldn't leave me, and yet here I am alone. After tonight I won't bother you guys ever again." Danielle got up and walked out of prom and walked and walked and walked.

Carl sat and watched Crystal and her date laugh and flirt. She was trying to make him jealous. Smirking like he had something up his sleeve. Rolling her eyes, Crystal stormed over to him. "What the hell are you looking at? And are you even supposed to be here?" She asks. "You'll see. And I got special permission and being supervised." He laughs. As Crystal walks away, a text message is sent to the student body.

Well, well, well… this isn't a new story but who is this girl in the video. I think we all know a certain jewel that was a part of Rose's clique. But one can only assume.

-TheDot.com

Video Attachment…

Everyone watched and laughed and looked around. Carl winked at Crystal as he watched his work. "Crys, is that you?" Amber asks as Crystal sat down. She pulled out her phone and opened the video. "Um, I'm gonna be right back." Crystal hurried to the bathroom. No one knew it was her for sure. Or did they? "Fuck you're so good at this.

Bend over." The distorted voice says. No faces were shown. That's the thing she never admitted it, and no one could ever prove it, but they all knew it was her, to Crystal it probably felt like they all knew too. That's the thing about society these days. Five people can feel like the whole world. She cried and cried. It wasn't like it hasn't happened before. But those were in middle school and freshman year and everyone that knew about it mostly graduated already except for some students that forced themselves to forget the image. She looked in the mirror at herself. How she changed. She touched her stomach and shook her head. "Game on." She whispered. She fixed her makeup and proceeded to her seat.

"Everything okay?" Trish asks. "Yeah, I watched it and thank god it wasn't me. I thought it could have been an old video or something. But that's not me." Crystal lied. "Who sent that out? Want me to fuck them up?" Vic whispered to her. "I don't know what you're talking about." She fixed her hair and blinked a few times to keep her tears back.

Jason sat in the locker room on the bench. Alone. Thinking if he should or should not do it. He bounced his knee anxiously. He tried to breathe slowly and count like his anger management coach taught him. "Fuck!" he screamed. Everything was coming together. *You are a freak. Just a game we played to see if you'd actually fall in love with me. You are pathetic. I never loved you and I never will. How could I ever really be with a freak like you?* The way Danielle treated him, the way she looks at the other guys, the way she said certain things, the things her friends said, the things his friends said. It was a game. He brought his hands to his head, revealing the gun. *No one likes you here.* That's when it happened. He snapped. He loaded the gun and started walking to the ballroom.

Nate entered through the back door of the locker room with Sarah. "Why are we here again?" Sarah asks. "To see if there is any evidence to help us with the investigation. Carl has to have something in here. Nate looked at the locker that was protected by a key lock. "Dammit! It's locked." He punches the locker. "Move over." Sarah pushed him and pulled out a bobby pin. "That doesn't actually work." Nate plopped onto the bench and dropped his head in his hands. Suddenly feeling a weight on his lap. "I was kidding." He laughs, shooting up from the bench.

They scavenged through the locker and came across a phone. There was a paper taped to the back that was titled, 'The Brotherhood.' Sarah turned it on and there were tons of videos on the phone of every girl that was involved dating back to the early 2000s. "This is it. This is our proof." Nate says. "Let's go. I need to find my sister." He added, running through the gym.

Danielle found her way in the girl's bathroom in the third building. She sat on the wall and cried. She lost everything. The perfect life she planned. The perfect reputation she had to rebuild. Her brother, her best friend. What else? She thought moving to a state would be an escape from her tarnished family name. She was wrong. Terribly wrong. Danielle walked to the sink and dried her face. The door started to open. The last person she wanted to see. The one who started all of this. "What do you want?" Danielle hissed. "I heard crying. I guess helping bad people is my skill." Spencer replies. "Do you really think I am a bad person?" Danielle asked. "No. I think you are hungry for attention. Self-absorbed. Materialistic but not a bad person. You just need to let that stuff go. It's not something you want to graduate with. It's fun for a while and then it destroys your life. I know because it happened to people I have seen grow up." Spencer explained, handing Danielle a tissue. "Thanks." Danielle fixed her makeup and reapplied her lips. She looks down at the red lipstick and handed it to Spencer. "It's a nice color. And it would look nice on you." Danielle flashed a smirk. "Did you just have a breakthrough?" Spencer laughed. "Maybe. Nerd." Danielle laughs. "Since you're pressing charges on Carl I will warn you. He has a team of lawyers. Be prepared for a war. That family is worse than mine. Yes my brother made his mistakes but that's not me. Enjoy your night." Danielle walks out.

Spencer enters the courtyard, making her way back to the ballroom. "Jason?" She called. He nervously stops in his tracks. "What are you doing here? I thought you weren't planning on coming." Spencer asks. "I just wanted to take care of a few things, that's all." Jason fakes a smile. In the window she sees the gun behind his back. "Well, prom is kind of boring. They haven't even played good music yet. Maybe they have. I just came because my mom wanted me to be a normal kid. But I'm going to go to my locker." Spencer made an excuse to leave. "Where did you just come from? Building three chem lab?" Jason asked. "I was checking to see if I left my book in there. But this week was so much with the police and investigation, I am exhausted." Spencer explained calmly. Jason looked over at building three and looked back at Spencer. "Have a good night. Nice lipstick." Jason smirked walking off.

Spencer walks into prom, now trembling. "Mr. English." She says, tears playing follow the leader down her cheeks. "What's going on?" Mr. English leaned in. "Jason went to building three. Danielle is in there." Spencer answered now crying. Peers are watching. Mr. English starts to storm off in a jealous rage until Spencer grabbed his arm. "Jason has a gun." She says.

  The loud music vibrates the windows as everyone dances on the dance floor. "You know, when they said prom will be held at school I thought it was going to suck. But it's actually really fun." Crystal says, taking a sip of her spiked punch. "Hello, earth to Amber. Are you listening?" Crystal snapped her fingers. "Sorry. I'm just thinking about Dani. What she said." Amber says, playing with her desert. "That bitch is a natural born liar. Don't worry about her." Crystal rolled her eyes. Amber stormed out into the courtyard. Trish and Crystal followed.

  "What is your problem?" Crystal yelled. "What is yours? Danielle did nothing to deserve any of this. We bullied her when all she wanted was friends." Amber yelled. "You better watch who you are talking to like that!" Crystal pointed at Amber. "Guys can we just stop?" Trish got between them. "Danielle is a liar. That's all she will ever be good at. Her good looks and lying. That will get her very far." Crystal barked. "You guys. I have information. A serious one." Bethany interrupted. "What are you wearing?" Amber said in a judgmental tone. "Shut up." Crystal snapped. "Spill it." Crystal ordered. "The night of the sleepover, Danielle snuck out of the penthouse. I followed her. She met this man and kissed him." She confessed. "So, we all do that once in a while. That's not information." Crystal rolled her eyes. "The man was Mr. English. I wasn't lying." Bethany added. "Still not a liar?" Crystal turned to Amber. "Let's find this little harlot and expose her." Crystal storms off to find her. "How about we just leave her alone? She didn't do anything to us!" Amber yelled. "What is your problem? You haven't been a good friend for a while. If you don't want to be friends then leave!" Crystal yelled back. "You know what. I've been here through everything. I'm sorry, I don't jump every time you need to talk about some random guy you fucked or new drug you tried. I raced over and held you on the bathroom floor while you cried. If that isn't a true friend then I guess we were never friends. Fuck our memories, fuck your fake feelings and fuck you Crystal!" Amber stormed off.

Danielle exits the bathroom and starts making her way down the hallway. "So, this was all a game to you?" She hears a voice in the side hallway. Jason. "Jason, please leave me alone." Danielle keeps walking. "You're all I have!" He yells. "No. I am not. We are in two different worlds. We would never have lasted. I did you a favor." Danielle argued back. "How? By cheating on me?" Jason asked. "What are you talking about?" Danielle asked, knowing exactly what he meant. "Tell me the truth." Jason now held the gun at her. "Jason. Put the gun down." Danielle yelled. "Tell the fucking truth!" Jason screamed. Eyes swollen from crying. Snot seeping from his nose like syrup. "God how could I be so fucking stupid! You tricked me. I love you Dani. So much. Why couldn't I be enough? Why can't I ever be enough?" Jason yelled. "You want the truth? I had a student teacher affair with Mr. English. It was wrong, but it happened. I tried to back away from him. I figured if I started dating someone he will leave me alone. And then I saw you. There was something about you that caught my eyes. You made me happy. But he wouldn't stop. I didn't want to be labeled as a girl that was hooking up with her teacher. I am sorry. But this isn't the answer Jason. I can't be with you because I am damaged. Always have been and always will be. I'm a freakin' mess." Danielle played the role well.

Around the corner, Mr. English was getting arrested from Danielle's confession. The other police waited for their moment. Nate and Sarah entered the hallway and stopped at the sight of the gun.

"What are you doing? Put that down bro!" Nate yelled with his hands up. "What are you doing here? You're not supposed to be here you rapist!" Jason then pointed the gun at Nate. "Jason no! Look at me. I'm here. Just focus on me." Danielle baited him back towards her. "You don't have to do this. You can build a future. You can be enough. Outside of this school. I never believed you couldn't." Danielle tried to talk him down. "You hurt me. A lot. Hurting you wouldn't do anything, but make me feel even worse." Jason says. A few moments passed and Jason aimed the gun toward Nate again. "But to get better, you have to get worse." Jason says. Gunshots echoed through the halls, mixing with Sarah and Danielle's screams. Another gunshot sounds. And another.

And another.

11. the eighth commandment

Day I.

They say the courtroom is one of the most serious places you will ever be in your life. Aside from the grave and in a hospital bed. They also say *You shall not bear false witness against your neighbor.* The Rose family sat in the front row in the courtroom. Judge Rollings takes his seat. "This is the case of **Carl Terril vs Spencer Loving.** We will be hearing this case a little differently." Rollings announced.

Carl sits at the front table with his three lawyers. Mr. McCormack stands from his seat. "I call **Miss Loving** to the stand." The lawyer swayed slowly over to the stand as she gave her oath. Spencer wore a navy-blue dress that fell to her knees with a white collared shirt underneath, like some school girl. Don't forget the blazer. Her hair curled down in front of her.

"Is it true that on the night of March15th, you were at the house party with Mr. Terril?" He asks. "Yes. I was invited." Spencer answered. "Invited by whom? If I may ask." Mr. McCormack held his hands behind his back. "Nathaniel Rose." Spencer started to tear up. "You stated and reported that you were sexually assaulted by my client. Is that true?" Mr. McCormack asks next. "Y-yes I was raped." Spencer answered in a quiet voice; barely anyone could hear her. The crowd leaned in, scooting to the edge of their seats. "Do you know the difference between sexual assault and rape, Miss Loving?" Mr. McCormack made a face at her answer. "Yes. Rape is penetration, assault is touching, grabbing or other forms of touching. Next question please." Spencer challenged him.

"Is it true that you willingly went into a bathroom with Mr. Terril at said house party?" Mr. McCormack continued. "You were the only one in the bathroom with him." He added in a low tone. Spencer lowered her head and nodded. "I'm sorry, but can you speak up, please." Mr. McCormack says. "I was helping him clean himself up after a drink was thrown on him." Spencer said, and she began to cry. The room started to buzz with whispers. "A drink that contained ketamine mixed with Rohypnol. Did you plan on drinking more with him?" Mr. McCormack asked. "No! I never had any intentions of that." Spencer yelled. "Order in my court." Judge Rollings demanded. "I have no further questions." Mr. McCormack said, walking away from the stand with a huge smile on his face.

Ms. Barnes, the other attorney, went up to the stand holding a piece of paper. "Can you please read what this says, Spencer. Loud enough so that the people in the back may hear you." She hands her the paper. Spencer sat up, wiped a few tears from her red eyes and read what was on the paper. "*I think you're really cute. I hope to one day be able to have a chance with you – Spencer Loving.*" She was shocked at the note. Ms. Barnes nodded and took back the paper. "This note was found in the textbook of Mr. Terril. It is possible that Spencer saw an opportunity at the party and took it. Then, not realizing what had happened, she came home, told her mother a lie, and reported it to the police." Ms. Barnes explained. "Are you saying I was taking advantage of Carl while he was drunk?" Spencer asked, angrily. "Those words never came out of my mouth Miss Loving." Ms. Barnes smiled. "Is it possible that he ignored this note and rejected you at the party?" She then asked. "No. Because I never wrote that. I know my handwriting. And that is not it." Spencer shot back. "It happens every day to young, beautiful girls. Why is it not possible for you?" Ms. Barnes asks. "Because he wasn't the one I had a crush on. Never have and never will. I saw he was drunk and struggling and decided to help him. That was my only mistake." Spencer replied. Ms. Barnes nodded and went back to her seat.

Mr. Haley then approached the stand. "Are you mentally ill? Are you sure you didn't write that note? Why did you leave a note instead of just telling him yourself?" He asks. "Objection!" Mrs. Myers proclaimed. "What relevance does my client's mental state have to the case?" She added. "Agreed." The judge said. "Mr. Haley, are you badgering the woman in order to confuse her?" Judge Rollings asks. Haley blinked his eyes innocently. "No, your Honor, I would never." He held his arms open. "Then, carry on." Judge Rollings continued. "I never wrote that note." Spencer glared towards Mr. Haley. "That is all." He went to take his seat. "Thank you, Miss Loving. I would like to call **Danielle** Rose to the stand." Mrs. Myers requested.

Danielle strutted up to the stand in her tight red dress and black blazer. "Miss Rose. Please dress appropriately for court." Judge Rollings comments. "Given what is in my closet, this is appropriate." Danielle answers with a smile. She flipped her orange curly hair behind her and crossed her legs. "Miss Rose, it was reported that you bullied Spencer Loving. Is that true?" Mrs. Myers asks. "Not at all. My former friends and myself gave her a makeover and helped her social skills in school. We did not bully her." Danielle answered. "That is not what the report says here." Mrs. Myers read the paper. "It says you and your brother, Carl, and your friends lured her there." Mrs. Myers pointed out. "Lured? I was not at the party, nor did I tell her to go. She wasn't ready for that scene. I was with my former boyfriend at the time." Danielle stated. "The boyfriend that brought a gun to prom? Rest his soul. The one you confessed to having a student teacher affair with Mr. George English to?" Mrs. Myers asked. Danielle raised an eyebrow. "Yes." She answers, looking at her family. "You also kept the knowledge of your brothers past a secret from her, putting her and your friends in potential danger. Is that correct?" Mrs. Myers added. "It's not my business to disclose with others. Especially when there are public resources online." Danielle commented back, now having an attitude. "But she was your friend. And you let that happen to her, was this something you planned with your brother?" Mrs. Myers asks. "Spencer and I created a new friendship." Danielle started. "My apologies, I was talking about Brielle Loft." Mrs. Myers corrected herself. "Don't you dare question my friendship or loyalty to Brielle. She was family to me." Danielle slammed on the stand. "Miss Rose. Control your temper." Judge Rollings ordered. "I guess what I am trying to get at is, why did Spencer go to that party? Where she was raped. Told by your own flesh and blood to go. Who has a past of such violent and aggressive nature. Danielle. Why did she go?" Mrs. Myers asks. "That should have been a question, to ask her. I am no one's keeper. I gave her a makeover. That was it." Danielle smirked. "She was your charity project. You took it upon yourself to change a girl whose life would have remained undisturbed. Did she ask you to change her?" Mrs. Myers asked, creeping closer to the stand. "She didn't, yet she didn't say no to it either. The new clothes, hair and makeup she liked it. She said this was a change that she needed. Sometimes people are scared to speak up or change because of the people around them. But, she didn't have any fear lying to the police about my brother and myself allegedly luring her to that party that we didn't attend. Funny how that works out. She had a lot to say at prom though. Hm." Danielle answered. "That is all Miss Rose." Ms. Myers took her seat, as did Danielle.

"We will continue this trial tomorrow morning at nine A.M. on the dot. Court dismissed." Judge Rollings banged the gavel.

Danielle got into the car with her family in an awkward silence. "Dad-" She started. "We will talk at home." He says with a stern tone. "Nate, when you get on that stand they are going to tear you apart. You need to be ready for anything that comes at you. I will be representing you. We will get past this." Donovan informs him, going through papers. "Nothing to worry about honey. We will be okay. Just keep your head up and out of the spotlight." Hazel says. "Hey, you okay?" Nate asked, placing his hand on Danielle's knee. "I'll be fine." She whispered as she caught a single tear on her cheek. "Kids, now you know how vicious lawyers can be. I hope this teaches you to not do anything that causes you to need one." Felton says, pulling into the driveway.

The family met in the living room. Danielle and Nate sat together on the couch, Felton in his favorite chair. Hazel and Donovan lingered in the back, feeling the anger building up in Felton. "How long has this been happening?" Felton asked. "Since the beginning of the school year." Danielle answered. "Did he..." Felton trailed off, interrupted by the thought of the two having sex. "No. Nothing like that happened. He flirted, I flirted. Maybe a kiss or two was exchanged. That was all." She explained, now crying. "He is an adult in an educational role! He is a pedophile." Felton punched the glass table, cracking it. "So you go to parties, do drugs, bully people in school, sleep with your teacher and you don't see that there's a serious issue?" Felton lists everything. "Sounds like I had a busy year this year." Danielle inspects her nails. "You just love to make our family look bad, don't you?" Felton asked. "You are a disgrace." He added. "Babe." Hazel says, shocked at the words coming from his mouth. Danielle's face hardened. "Yes. I am. Next to rapists and killing friends in a failed attempt to get their businesses, I am a huge disgrace. I always looked up to you daddy. How you worked, how you made things happen. How you socialized. I was amazed. Now, I see a failure. A failure of a businessman, a failure of a man and a failure of a father." Danielle hit him in the softest part. "Dani!" Donovan snapped. Shocked at his daughter's reply, Felton let a tear drop. "Look at that. Now we are both hurt. Hope it was worth it." Danielle strutted to her room.

Dinner was awkward and silent. Nate received a text message. He looked at it under the table. "No phones at the dinner table." Hazel reminded him. "Sorry mom." He says, turning down the brightness.

Unknown : Control your bitch or this picture will be used tomorrow.

Attachment: 1 Image

Someone had a picture of Nate and Elijah the night of the party. "I have to go." Nate dashed out of the house and into the car. "Erica! Are you home?" He asked in a panic. "Yes. Why?" She replies. "What is wrong?" She added. "I'm on my way." Nate hangs up.

Erica waited outside of her home, pacing nervously. She sees the car pull up in the driveway and Nate jumps out. "What is going on?" She asks, kissing him. "Carl sent this to me. If you testify tomorrow, he will release this picture. I can go to jail." Nate informed her. "Nate. I will not let him get away with rape. I let that football team and a bully destroy my sister and she is dead. I will not let that happen to this girl." Erica replied, her voice getting louder with anger. "I can't go to jail." Nate says. "I ignored your past. And now you want me to protect another rapist? Leave! Now!" Erica stormed to the door. Nate grabbed her arm and pushed her against the front glass door. "Please!" He whispers, realizing he was losing his temper. "Goodbye." She says, walking into the house.

Day II.

    Court was in session for the continuation of the trial. Judge Rollings entered and got settled in his chair. The room is silent as he takes a sip of water, everyone waiting on his instruction. "Let's start." He says. "Your honor, I'd like to call **Crystal** Lopez to the stand." Mrs. Myers announced. Crystal walked up to the stand. "Miss Lopez, you are friends with Danielle Rose correct?" Mrs. Myers asks. "Were friends." Crystal corrected. "Oh, mind if I ask why did the friendship end?" Mrs. Myers turned towards Danielle. "No one wants to be friends with a girl whose brother is a rapist. So, we all stopped talking to her." Crystal explained. "Within good reason." Mrs. Myers comments. "Has she ever forced you to bully or torment another student?" She added. "She's a classic mean girl. We all decided to give Spencer a makeover though. And Spencer never rejected it." Crystal explains. "Thank you." Mrs. Myers says, then calls **Amber** who explained the same thing and nothing but good experiences with the Rose family.

Finally, Mrs. Myers calls **Erica** to the stand. "Miss Worthington. How was your experience with Nathaniel?" She asks, looking through a folder. "He is my boyfriend. He has been nothing but nice to me. But what does he have to do with what Carl did at the party?" Erica asks. "What do you know about the party?" Mrs. Myers changes topics. "I was told not to go by my boyfriend. He told me Carl isn't a good guy. I should have listened. I saw Carl put something in a drink and gave it to me. I poured it into his cup and asked to go to the bathroom just to get away from him. That could have been me in there. He had me follow him to this room where I saw these other girls and guys from the football team having sex. I am not sure if the girls were drugged or not. I took a book of names, and inside I found my sister's name. I threw the drink on Carl and ran out of the room and apparently bumped into Spencer on the way out. I didn't know her or that she would have that happen to her." Erica explained. "Wow. You drugged Mr. Terril, in hopes of what? Getting revenge for your sister? Or what?" Mrs. Myers asks. "Did they teach you your great listening skills in law school? He tried to drug me. That would have been me on that bathroom floor." Erica answers. "So, you took it upon yourself to take matters into your own hands, did it ever occur to you that Miss Loving wouldn't be in this position if you would have just said no and left?" Mrs. Myers asked. "I wasn't thinking about her because I didn't know her. I didn't know he would even do something like that." Erica started to cry. "That's all your honor." Mrs. Myers took a seat.

Mr. McCormack walked up to the stand. "You confess you contributed to the alleged attack of Miss Loving?" He asks. "Excuse me? Absolutely not!" Erica yelled. "You raped that girl! How many girls have you raped? Sorry had sex without content. Because In your book it showed the number ten next to your name. If I have to expose every single person in that book, then so be it." Erica yelled. "Do not address my client at any point!" Mr. McCormack yelled over her. Judge Rollings tried to gain control over her. "And that is the truth, under oath." Erica smirked. "That's all for today." Mr. McCormack gathered his papers and stormed to the judge to ask something.

Erica washed her face with water in the bathroom sink as the door opened. "Hey you." Danielle appeared. "Hey. You just don't care about court dress code, do you?" Erica laughed. "No one tells me what I can and can't wear. I don't care what authority they think they have. A job can always be taken from someone." Danielle fixed her makeup. "Nate didn't want me to testify today." Erica confesses. "Why?" Danielle shot a look at her. "Carl sent him a picture. Blackmailing him and threatening me. The picture was about tha-" Danielle covered Erica's mouth as she saw the heels under the stall. "Someone is in here." She mouthed. "I think those ten girls that are in the book should speak out within the next twenty-four hours. And I know just where to find them." Danielle lies, strutting out with Erica.

Meeting up with her family, Danielle overheard Felton talking to someone on the phone. "Who was that daddy?" She asks. "A lawyer. Now if you don't mind I need to see your brother." Felton hurries off, still embarrassed by her actions.

Later that night, Erica and her mother walked up to the front door of her home with grocery bags when they heard tires screeching on the road. She turns to see people in a red truck. They start throwing eggs at her and her mother. Her mother struggles to get her keys in the door before they are completely covered in eggs. Rotten eggs. Her mother gathers up the groceries off of the floor, crying. Anger. No, rage builds up inside of Erica. Something in her mind whispered to her. "Do it."

Well, well, well. We have something new and different. A list of names. This is a special list that the football players of

Oberlin High created. The girls they have hooked up with, drugged and recorded. I guess we know why Romeo and Juliet broke up. Troy and Sarah. I am so shocked I can't breathe. The Tea is too hot right now! To make it short, I will only do the most recent names. They are the ones that matter right now. #METOO

Love- TheDot.com

<u>The Smash List</u>:
Jenna - Leroy(6)
Iris- John, Ben, Sam
Ebony- John(2), Terry
Jeniffer- Preston, Terry(3)
Pricilla- Marcus, Tim
Monica- Jake, Ben, John
Avrey-Mike, Carl
~~Annabella - Troy~~
~~Bryanna- Grayson~~
Carissa-
Sarah W- Troy, Mike, John(2), Carl(10), Dave, John(4),Ben.
Ashleigh-
Amy-
Cassie- Jet
Spencer- Carl

Erica did it. She exposed the very people that hurt her family. It wasn't Annabella running Sarah out of town. It wasn't her parents forcing them to change their lives. It was the jocks that took advantage of Sarah. Then a text came through.

Nate: *What the hell did you do!*

Day III

The final day of the trial and it was time to hear **Carl** and Nate's testimonies. The jury gathered in their seating area, the audience in their seats. And **Nathaniel** on the stand. Carl's lawyers gather like vultures getting ready to tear this innocent boy apart. "Mr. Rose. How did you meet Spencer?" Mr. McCormack asked. "She was friends with my sister. I did not know her prior to the night of the party." Nate answered. "Enough to invite her to a party." Mr. McCormack added. "I never invited her. I asked if she was going. She said she wasn't planning on it. She then asked me if I was going and I told her I might make an appearance. I was standing next to my girlfriend when saying this, so I didn't lead her on in any way." Nate defended himself. "So, you tricked her into thinking you will be there. Why didn't you show up? If I may ask." Mr. McCormack asked next. "I was at the police station being questioned." Nate looked around. "Okay. For the murder of Elijah Ethans?" Mr. McCormack stepped closer. "Relevance." Nate's lawyer; Mr. Tejada yelled to the judge. "This is not a trial for alleged murder

Mr. McCormack. Please move this along." Judge Rollings informed. Donovan whispered something to Tejada. "My apologies. You were being questioned on an alleged murder. And after? This wasn't some kind of set up between you and your girlfriend?" Mr. McCormack changed the question. Nate took a deep breath, balling up his fist in his lap. "I went home. With my father. No! Absolutely not. I would never set anyone up." Nate answers. "So, you are saying you didn't trick Miss Loving. You didn't lure her, and you didn't know her. Your girlfriend confessed to drugging Carl. How do we know this even happened? How do we know you are telling the truth? Why are we here?" Mr. McCormack sounded annoyed. "Because I was on the football team and a football player allegedly raped her. I know Carl. I have spent months with him, games, locker room, school, even slept over his house and hung out after school." Nate started to explain. He and Carl made eye contact. "I don't know him to be a rapist." Nate added. "You can go back to your seat now Mr. Rose." Mr. McCormack walked to the table.

Mrs. Myers stepped up. "I would like to call Carl up to the stand." Carl walks up with a confident smirk on his face. "Do you swear to tell the truth, the whole truth and nothing but the truth?" The bailiff asks as Carl holds up his right hand. "I do." He says. He takes a seat at the stand and looks out into the sea of people that are watching his every move. Untouchable he calls himself. "The night of March 15th did you attend and host a party at your residence?" She asks. "Yes. I threw a party that night to celebrate our winning game." Carl agreed. "And at this party, were there drugs and alcohol present?" She asks next. "If there was, I had no part in it. As you heard before, I was drugged." Carl smiles. "Correct. From a drink that you were giving to Miss Worthington. So, you drugged yourself in a way." Mrs. Myers connected the dots. "Leading." Mr. McCormack yelled. "Mrs. Myers move on please." Judge Rollings says. "Did you have a sexual encounter with Miss Loving?" Mrs. Myers asked, pacing back and forth. "I don't know." Carl replies. "Did you have sex without consent with Miss Loving or any other girls on this list?" Mrs. Myers pulled up the post on the screen. "We had no information about this your honor." Mr. McCormack slammed the file on the table. "I submitted them in last night. Had you been available when I reached out, you would have been aware." Mrs. Myers explained. "Continue Mrs. Myers." judge Rollings says.

"So, Mr. Terril, did you?" She turned back to him. He knows now he was not untouchable. He looked at the jury and over in the audience. "We went to a party out of the city. Nate was fighting Elijah and killed him. The body fell into the water and sunk. We took Nate to my house and washed him off. He begged me not to tell and said he would let me be Captain." Carl let a tear fall down his cheek. "Mr. Terril. That has nothing to do with this case, this girl wanted a friend. She thought those girls were her friends. Instead she was raped. Not by a stranger. By someone she saw in trouble and needed help. You were roofied at your party and she tried helping you and you destroyed this girl's life forever. These girls are unaware of what happened to them. Why?" Mrs. Myers started yelling. "Your honor!" Mr. McCormack yelled.

Then it happened. It all came out, crashing like the waves into the sharp rocks. "It was tradition. We had to do it. Every football player that wants to be respected has to. I was angry and not in control of my body. I am so sorry. I didn't mean to." Carl confessed. "That is all." Mrs. Myers walked back to the table and sat next to Spencer. "I told you I will get him." She whispered. "The jury will make their decision and we will regroup when the jury has made their decision." Judge Rollings banged the gavel.

Spencer sat in the lobby wrapped in her mother's arms. "Everything will be okay." Her mother kissed her forehead. "Hey, how are you feeling?" Danielle came over and hugged her. "I feel better. I feel calmer." Spencer started. "Can you leave us alone. You have done enough." Her mother snapped. "What have I done exactly? Get your daughter to feel comfortable in the clothes she actually wanted? Get her comfortable enough to be around her fellow peers? She is a teenager. Let her live a little. I know given the recent events that is not likely to happen, but I wanted to help her be the person she is." Danielle started off. "You know, everyone calls me selfish and conceited, but I am not. I love who I am, I am confident in who I am. I know who I am." Danielle added before leaving the area.

Mr. McCormack started packing up his things. "What are you doing?" Mrs. Terril asked. "When the other lawyers walked off of the case, I thought they were foolish. I thought they didn't understand the case like I did. Your son got on that stand and made a fool out of me." Mr. McCormack explained angrily. "I am sorry. I just had to tell the truth. I can't lose everything I built this year." Carl replies. "You already lost it all!" Mr. McCormack barked. "Sir." A man walked over to them. "What!" Mr. McCormack yelled at him. "The jury is back." He hesitantly replied.

12. All the Good Girls Go To Hell.

Well, it was time. After scrapping Nathaniel's testimony from the trial due to what was confessed, the jury came back with their decision. The room was awkwardly silent. The air was thin. Spencer sat at the front table. Knee length dress that was the color of the sky. Her hands fidgeting in her lap. Her breathing gets heavier. She closes her and takes deep breaths. *Calm down Spence. It will be okay, she* tells herself. Carl bounced his foot, knowing his world will soon come crashing down. How did this happen? How did he get caught up in this "frat boy" lifestyle? He lets out a deep sigh. He looks up to his mother. She can't look at him, not after the confession. Not after what he did. All she could think about was how much of a monster he was. The stranger living in her home all these years. He reaches for her hand, but before he could feel the soft skin on her hand, she placed them in her lap. "Before we get to the jury, I would like to say Mr. Terril you are very strong to do what you did up there today." Judge Rollings smirked. "Let's hope the jury thinks so also. It is time for the verdict." He added.

"We find the defendant; Carl Terril." The woman stood up and read from the paper. She didn't try to dress the part. Her blond curly hair peeked out from under her bandana like she just got finished gardening. She has the power to put Carl away for life. "Not guilty." She says. Those words. Those fucking words. Those words that crashed into

Spencer's world and lit it on fire. A sigh of relief expelled from Carl's body and through that smile. Spencer burst into tears and stormed out of the courtroom. Danielle and the other girls after her.

Spencer locked herself in the stall and just cried her heart out. Cried the hardest she ever could. "Spence. Come out please." Danielle knocked. "Please just go away." She yelled. "No. We want to make sure you are okay." Crystal replied. "We are not leaving. Even if I have to sit on this floor and wait." Danielle stomped her foot. "Please don't make me get on the floor, it's so gross." Danielle danced a bit in her Gianvito Rossi heels. Letting out a sigh, Danielle sat on the cold bathroom floor. Pulling down her black dress, she got comfy. "At least open the door." Amber commented. Spencer opened the door to see them there. "If we were not your friends, we wouldn't be here." Crystal says. "Thank you, guys." Spencer forced the words out. Eye liner dripping down her face. Danielle hopped up and hugged her tightly. "It will be okay. Just gotta keep your head up." Danielle held her close as Spencer's mother entered the room. "He will get his. Eventually. We will make sure of it." Crystal added. "No girls. Revenge isn't the answer. It will only stir up more mess." Spencer's mother commented. "This will be a new chapter for you Honey. We will move and start new. Where no one can treat you differently." She added. "Come on, let's go." Spencer and her mother left the bathroom. The courthouse and eventually, the city.

Felton has one last piece left in this game of chess with Bryanna. If she learned anything from Annabella, it was to always have your soldiers ready. Bryanna has her policemen and her horseman protecting her. Felton was sure he could get her with one man. "Conall." Felton calls out to the man. He is tall and dressed in a navy-blue suit. His shoes were black and shiny. He wore a ring on just about every finger. "I was wondering if I'd ever hear from you again. Tell me, why travel all this way to meet?" Conall asks, sitting down at the park bench. "I have a problem. A Dayton problem." Felton answers, pulling a folder out. "Ah, the little Dayton. I heard about her. She is a clever one." Conall laughs. "That bitch took my house, my company, my reputation." Felton stopped and took a breath. "If I can't have it, none of us can." Felton raises an eyebrow. "As long as you have my Irish blood in your veins, I will make sure the job is taken care of." Conall answers. "Thank you dad." Felton smiles. "I will do you this favor. The FBI is after you. Stay low. They have a lot on you. They don't need anything else against you." Conall vanished through the park.

Bryanna sits on the Rachel Veil talk show to talk about her life, career and recent book. "How did you feel in prison? Why did you run?" Rachel asks. "I needed to make sure my daughter was in the right hands. So I took her to close family and turned myself in. After hearing on the news about my parents and my sisters." Bryanna pauses and started to sob, soon turning into full on crying. "I'm sorry. It really still hurts. I never really got a chance to mourn properly or even say goodbye." Bryanna wiped her tears with the tissue. "We will be back."

Rachel cut to commercial. "Take as much time as you need." Rachel hugged Bryanna.

Bryanna took a minute backstage and thought about the next move.

"We are back after a very emotional moment, Bryanna. Tell us what happened." Rachel turned to Bryanna. "My parents were betrayed over The H Hotel. They were murdered by a hitman sent by Felton Rose. My sister was married for a few hours before being held hostage by a man that was getting revenge on us for the explosion that was unknowingly caused by her. My other sister committed suicide to get away from all of this. My family has withered away like petals on a rose. I decided to take up ownership over The H Hotel because it is my legacy as the surviving Dayton. It is my daughter's legacy. And women are more aggressive than a man could ever be." Bryanna smiled. "You are so strong and have been through so much. Past is the past and you did time for it. Many people out there and I are indeed rooting for you. And all can be found in her new book *Beautiful Wicked*. Thank you for coming and showing the world who you really are." Rachel hugged Bryanna. "When you leave, go out the left door and get into a different car." She whispered and shared a warning look.

The interview was finished, and Bryanna did as she was told. Seeing her, her driver started her car and in seconds it was engulfed in flames. She looked around and saw an orange rose by the door. "Okay. You want to see a flame. I'll show you flames." She whispered, storming into the car. "What is the plan?" Ben asked. "We act soon. We show them who we are. Call Michael. Inform him of what happened. I need the name of the hit man or men after me. I know Felton doesn't get his hands dirty. But I do." Bryanna tries to calm her mind.

Me: *Thank you.*

Rachel: *Us women have to stick together.*

Rachel: *video attachment:*

There he was. The bald man ordered a young man to tamper with the car. No masks. Irish. "I've seen this man before. At one of my parents' parties when I was a kid." Mike says. "Find them and get rid of them. Put an orange rose with them since they like to leave those laying around. No jackets and cover your faces." Bryanna ordered.

She then called the detective and let her and the police know what happened. "You need evidence in order to convict someone. Otherwise everyone and their mother will be taking people to court that they don't like then. Get me Proof." She says.

Staring at the phone, Bryanna sent the video to the news station.

Nate knew something bad was about to happen. He knew someone was coming. "How much for it?" Nate asks the man. Standing in an alley in Brooklyn. "Eight hundred." He says. The man was tall but not taller than Nate. He was Spanish with a rough voice. He had tattoos on his face. He looked as if he would kill Nate at any moment. "Here's a thousand." Nate handed him the money. "Damn you must really be in trouble. You know how to shoot it?" The man asks. "I'm a pro. Just need to protect myself from some people." Nate aimed the nine-millimeter at the ground. Fake shooting the grass. "My name is Vortex. Pleasure doing business with you." Vortex shook his hand.

Nate made it back to the city in the town car. Gripping the book bag. Shaking his leg nervously. "Mr. Rose is everything okay?" The driver asks. "Yes. Just thinking about everything." Nate answered. "I'm just making sure. I wasn't happy about you buying drugs from that man." The driver replied. "Tony, I promise I was not buying drugs." Nate looked up into the rear-view window. "Take me to The H Hotel please." Nate ordered.

Making his way into the hotel, Nate goes to his usual spot on the roof. He could think and breathe. He wasn't worried about anything. He knew what would happen next. Just like last time, they pack up and move away from their problems. "I hope you're not going to jump." Erica lets out a snicker. "Debating it." Nate doesn't take his eyes away from the view. "I am sorry. What I did was done out of anger. He was supposed to go to jail. When I saw my sister's name and then the eggs I had to do it." Erica tried to explain. "What you did was stupid and reckless. You not only put yourself in danger, you put me in danger too." Nate yelled. He could feel himself getting angry. He could feel himself losing who he was. "Carl was supposed to go to jail." Erica starts crying. That doesn't faze Nate. Not this time. Not anymore. "Guys like Carl do not get jail time. Guys like Carl gets off and gets to live their lives." Nate stepped closer to her. "You mean guys like you?" Erica comments in a moment of sudden anger. And that was it. Nate gripped her neck and pinned her against the wall. "You are fucking dead to me." He whispered. "The difference between me and Carl, I made a mistake and lived every day dying on the inside knowing I hurt the girl that I could see my future with. He never cared and never will." Nate let her go and stormed into the hotel. All Erica could do was fall to the ground and cry.

Felton and Hazel walks out of the lawyer's office. "What do we do now?" Hazel asks crying. "You start your life Ms. McVan. I transferred all of my assets to you so that you're not struggling. You are a very wealthy woman who married a murderer. And you had nothing to do with it. I love you and I will always love you. I hope our paths cross again one day. I am so sorry for this." Felton hugged her close and gave her one last kiss. "Mr. Rose." The FBI agent called. Felton knew what had to be done. He put his hands behind his back and held his head up high. "You are under arrest for the murder of Julian and Charlotte Dayton and the attempted murder of Bryanna Dayton." The agent started to read him his rights but the only thing he could do was stare at Hazel. His now ex-wife. She hurried to the car before the paparazzi showed up.

"Danielle are you with Nate?" Hazel asks crying. "No. Mom what's wrong?" Danielle asks. "Your father. He was arrested for murder and will be going away for a while. I will explain later. Just be safe please." Hazel says hanging up the phone. She drives to the beach and sits in the sand. The sun hitting her skin. The waves crashing on the shore. The breeze calming her mind. There was only one place like this. She missed for so long. She opened her eyes. "It's time to go home." She whispers.

When the sun started to go down, Hazel made it to a bar in the Upper East Side. "A martini please." She ordered. "Long day I see." A man in a royal blue suit commented. He was handsome. Long, chiseled face looked like something Michelangelo would create, slim but muscular. Short brown hair that was well maintained. He was young but knew his business. His smile was warming. They talked and had multiple intellectual conversations and shared laughs. "So, what is your story?" He asks. She looked at the TV and saw the news report about her husband's arrest. "I got divorced today. And I guess I am just starting my life today. I settled down too young and was in a stressful marriage." Hazel fixed her eyes on him. "I hope I can take your mind off of it." He places his hand on hers. "I think you can." She smiled. "Let's head back to my place. I have a pretty nice guest house I would love to play in." She bites her lip. He helps her out of her seat and kisses her hand.

After driving around for over an hour, Danielle finally sees Nate. "Hey loser. Get in the fucking car." Danielle yells out of the window.

13. EMBERS AND DIAMONDS.

Carl walks into his kitchen with Lucas laughing and joking about the case. "Carl get in here." His father yells. Carl walks into the living room to see a crying Crystal and her angry parents. "Lucas this is a family matter. Please go home." Mr. Terril orders. "See you man." Lucas pats Carl and hurried out. "How long have you known about this young woman's pregnancy?" Mr. Terril asks. "Not long." Carl lies. "Tell the truth. Now. There is no more room for secrets." Mr. Terril grabs Carl by the neck. "He found out he had an STD and blamed me. We hooked up a lot throughout the school year and I went to get tested and I was clean, but I was pregnant. That was two months ago." Crystal starts crying. "You will take care of this child. You will be responsible for your actions. You want to be a man. That's what men do." Mr. Terril yells.

The parents gather in the kitchen to figure out what to do next. "You just want to ruin my life." Carl couldn't make eye contact with her. Crystal sat next to him. "Carl. You are a real asshole. I have a heart of gold and just wanted to feel loved. I fell in love with a guy who kept me a secret because of my weight. Who constantly put me down and hurt me. The sex wasn't even that great. Just good enough and easily accessible." Crystal pulled his face closer for one last kiss. And in that moment Carl felt something. Something like love. "Don't worry. I won't have this baby. The father of my child won't be anything like you. I promise." Crystal gets up and walks into the kitchen to get her parents.

After fighting the crowd of protesters outside, and unknowingly passing Amber, Crystal and her mother wait in the clinic, waiting to be called. Sometimes the decisions we make affect everything around us. How people look at us. What they think about us. What they will wish for us.

Amber: *"Hey where are you?*
Crys: *I have something to take care of. TTYL*

"It will be okay." Mrs. Lopez said, kissing Crystal's hand. "I am so sorry. For all of this. It wasn't supposed to happen. I was just lonely and sad. I never felt loved." Crystal says, wiping a tear from her cheek. "486." They called. "We will talk after." Her mother kisses her forehead.

Crystal followed the nurse into the room and laid on the table. "You'll feel a slight pinch, I promise it is normal." The nurse says in a calm voice. Crystal grips the sides of the table and breathes in. After a short time, it was over. That part of her life was in the past. What could have been was no longer. She only had a future to build with Vic. Who loved her and showed her how she should be treated. What she deserved, true happiness.

Amber sits in the psychiatrist's office with her parents and little brother. She sits tensed in the teal chair while Chase plays on the floor with toys and her parents sits on the couch. Tiffany sitting close enough to make it look like things are somewhat getting better. "Amber, tell me and your parents what you are thinking." She says in a calming voice. The room smelled like vanilla, it was soothing. Amber took a few deep breaths. "Dad, for a while you have been getting worse and worse. Your drinking started getting out of hand and then you became aggressive and then came violence. I do not feel safe with you in the house anymore. For the sake of my life and my little brother. He is scared. I am terrified to come home sometimes. I cry myself to sleep. I wake up extra early to put makeup over the bruises. I am tired." Amber explained. "We can't live like this anymore. I understand you are still hurting over uncle's death. You were angry at him for so long and didn't get a chance to say goodbye to him. But that was over two years ago. We have been waiting for a change and I have given up waiting." Tiffany hands him a folder. "I am leaving. This time I am taking my kids. Sign the papers." She says. He sits there in shock with the rest of the room. "I can change. I can get better. I promise. I will go to AA, I will never drink again." He begs her. "Honey, I love you. Please." He adds. "You have said that eight times throughout the year and I gave you chance after chance. I am over it. Please sign them." Tiffany replies. With a sudden burst of rage, he signs. "Thank you." Tiffany packs her things. "Let's go kids." Amber picks up Chase and walks to the door. "Show me you will change. Until then, my children are not safe with you." Tiffany shut the door. "Marcus. I did not see that coming." The psychiatrist says. "She was always one for the dramatics. Thank you." He crawls out of the office. The pain he felt was unbearable and most definitely unexpected.

Danielle made it to Evverruns Path Woods with Nate and parked in the lot. "Dani, why are we doing this?" Nate sighs. "Closure. Make sure this chapter of my life is finished. Just stay here please." Danielle explained getting out of the car. She started off into the woods. The creek was close, she could hear the spring water. There he was. In the distance, that tall slim man. His orange hair brought out his pasty skin and blue eyes. Danielle could admit he was handsome. His smile said one thing but the look in his eyes said another. Danielle tucks her hair behind her ear and gives a smile. "You look so beautiful." George compliments her, examining her body. She tugged her skirt down a bit. "Thank you. You look very handsome." She replied. Something wasn't right. Something was off about him. She took a step back as he took one forward. "Why did you want to meet here?" She asks. "I wanted to see you. I can't stop thinking about you. I can't stop wanting you. I crave you Danielle." He explained. "I just want you to know I didn't tell on you." Danielle confesses. "I know. I know you didn't." He smiles. "I think we shouldn't do this anymore. It's not safe." Danielle says, backing up again. That's when it happened. The gun pointed at her.

"You want to end it? This special bond we have. You aren't going anywhere." George hissed.

"Get over there. Now!" He yells. His voice echoes through the woods. Danielle does as instructed for once. She stands in front of the stream. "Take your clothes off." His voice is unrecognizable. "Please. Don't do this." She starts crying. George walks over and nearly rips her clothes off. "If you scream, I'll fucking kill you." He whispered as he turned her around. She felt something hard. Press against her. This isn't what she wanted. She wanted to flirt and have fun like before. Not this. "I gave up my career for you. It's your turn to give up something for me now. You have played and teased me all year. You little slut. You will get what I give you. What a man gives you." He says, unzipping his pants. Danielle sees an opportunity and disarms him. The gun goes into the river. "You stupid bitch!" He yells, now gripping her hair and dragging her to the water. He holds her head under for just a moment. "I'm going to give you the time of your life." He turns her over and spreads her legs. "Help!" She screams, hoping her brother would hear her. She screams and kicks and repeats it until she is on her feet. Nate followed the screams and tackled George to the ground. "Stay the fuck away from my sister!" He says, punching and punching and punching. Danielle makes it over to the river in searches for the gun. Frantically searching in the water until she heard a shot go off.

George stood there, shocked. Speechless. When he coughed, blood started dripping from his mouth. The gun in Nate's hands trembled. "I... I had to." Nate started to panic. "Don't. It is okay. I need you to get that bullet out of him. Clean up in the river." Danielle orders him. *Rose, get in the water.* Nate shook the thought out of his head and ran over to George and looked for the entry wound. Danielle puts up her curly wet hair and helps him find it. She sticks the bullet in her bra. "Help me move the body into the river." She says. "What? We will get in more trouble. I already have a case against me." Nate panicked. "No body. No case." Danielle looked at him. "Please." She whispered. Nate looked down at his sister and saw something genuine for the first time in a very long time. He helps drag the body into the creek. And they returned to the car and drove to the beach.

Handing Danielle her Starbucks drink, Nate sat next to her in the warm sand. "Thank you for saving me." Danielle says through the tears. "You're my sister. I will always save you." Nate walked behind her and held her. "I know you hate me. I know I ruined all of our lives. But just know I love you so much and I would never do anything to intentionally hurt you." Nate rested his chin on her shoulder, watching the waves come in.

Bryanna,Ben and Michael met. Bryanna strutted up to the Rose mansion in her sister's famous Louboutin's. She looked through the glass door, but no one was home. No staff. No pets. Learning some skills in prison, Bryanna picked the lock and was in. Her heels clicked into the kitchen as Ben took apart the pipe to the gas stove, exposing gas into the air. Bryanna and Michael trailed gas from the front door. "I lost everything. My family. My life." Bryanna flicked a match into Nathaniel's bedroom trash can.

The three stood in front and watched as the house burned and then exploded. "The men were taken care of. What is next?" Michael asks. "We return to Georgia." Bryanna smiles, walking to the car. Neighbors come pouring out of their homes and sirens appear in the distance. The Dayton legacy has been restored. The war was won. Bryanna will expand her father's work and build the empire not only for her, but for her daughter too. Ben and Michael will go back to their regular lives. She never understood why her sister always felt so good after winning a take down, until this very moment.

"Miss Rose. This is serious. Someone was killed amongst other events that happened. What do you know about it?" The investigators asked. Danielle sat in the chair, arms and legs crossed. "His body was found in the river. Given your recent relationship with the victim, it is important for us to discredit any possible suspects. Please." The investigator slides a picture of the corps. A tear fell from Danielle's puffy red eyes. "I want my lawyer." She demands. "You're not in any trouble or anything. We just need the truth." He says. "The truth is he was a creep. He watched me at lunch, he kept me after class, he followed me home and hanging out with my friends. He was always there. I'm sure he was doing it to other girls too. That is the truth. I didn't kill him. And after he tricked me into preforming sexual acts I really just want to forget and move on." Danielle started crying. "You may go. I apologize if we triggered any traumatic feelings." The other investigator said, opening the door. Danielle walked out of the police station with her smile and her curly orange hair bouncing with every step. "You ready sis?" Nate asked opening the car door for her. "As ready as I'll ever be." Danielle winks.

"The autopsy report shows Elijah Ethans died from drowning. Even though Mr. Rose defended himself from this boy who assaulted him. My client did not kill him." The lawyer says.

The Rose's relocated to a new city and state. New lives. To start over. Los Angeles, California. Hazel was still healing from the explosion. Nate and Danielle finally moving on from everything that happened. Nate and Danielle struts into a random house party that was in full affect. Wearing a white one shoulder mini dress from CB. "Did you really think you could have a party without inviting moi?" Danielle smiles at everyone. "Who are you?" A girl strutted over to her. "I am the new girl. Seeing if your parties are up to my standards. Danielle but everyone calls me Dani." Danielle smiles. Danielle catches a glimpse of herself in the mirror and sees other people staring. "I look like a fucking goddess. You know, from the gossip that's being spread right now." Danielle says, fixing her makeup. "Your standards? You wish you were that important." The girl laughs as she walks off with her posse. "Listen up fives, a ten is speaking. By the time school ends, you all will know who I am. I hope you can handle the heat." Danielle explains. The lights went out and black lights came on, revealing all the neon colors on the guests. Everyone danced and drank and smoked. The music was euphoric. Aside from the smoke from weed floating around the room and the couples nearly having sex on the dance floor, she saw a group of guys in the corner. "What are you guys up to?" She asked flirtatiously. "Just a little fun." The blond guy replied, licking his perfect white teeth. "I like to have fun too." Danielle pulled out a tiny bag of molly. "What is it?" He asks as she crushed the pills. "I thought we were having fun." She winked. She made two lines and rolled her hundred-dollar bill. Colorful lasers danced around the room. White lights strobed to the beat of the music. They both sniffed the lines and smiled at each other. "Let's dance." She pulled him onto the dance floor to the song Conga by Gloria Estefan. There was something about her that he liked. Everyone looks at the two. They watched as if she was dancing with the most popular guy in school. Little did she know... she was. Not a care in the world. New life, same game. She turned and kissed him. "I don't even know your name." He smiled, holding her close. "You will." She kissed him again and took a blunt out of rotation.

"We find the defendant, Nathaniel Rose innocent for the murder of Elijah Ethans." The jury announced.

The next morning, Dani enters Starbucks and sips on her drink with Nate. Her *House of CB* bags piled on the floor next to her. Then she sees them. At some point in life you make a choice about who you want to be and what you want in life. At the moment, Danielle made that choice. She walks over and sits with them in the booth. Nate watching everything from the table. "You girls seem like an interesting group. You all go to school around here?" Danielle asks, smiling.

CHARACTERS

DANIELLE ROSE	NATHANIEL ROSE
FELTON ROSE	HAZEL ROSE*
DONOVAN ROSE	BRYANNA DAYTON
BEN DAYTON	MRS. RADCLIFFE
ERICA WORTHINGTON	AMBER WEATHERSFIELD
CRYSTAL LOPEZ	TRISH SAMPSON
MICHAEL DAYTON	JASON MERRIT*
XIN CHAO	CONNER WARREN
SPENCER LOVING	DETECTIVE WILSON
GEORGE ENGLISH*	EMILY DARKO
JASMINE FORTELLE	LUCAS
DEVON MORRIS	DETECTIVE BENNINGS
DETECTIVE JOHNSON	ELIJAH ETHANS
DETECTIVE JONES	CARL TERRIL
MRS. MYERS	MR. HALEY
MS. BARNES	MR. MCCORMACK
JUDGE ROLLINGS	BRIELLE LOFT
RACHEL VEIL	VORTEX
CHANEL ST. JAMES RADCLIFFE-DAYTON	
MAXIM CHERNOV	ELIZABETH ROSE
CONALL ROSE	BETHANY
DALLAS	MARSHALL DUDLEY